Walter Jerrold

Oliver Wendell Holmes by Walter Jerrold

With a portrait

Walter Jerrold

Oliver Wendell Holmes by Walter Jerrold
With a portrait

ISBN/EAN: 9783743303461

Manufactured in Europe, USA, Canada, Australia, Japa

Cover: Foto ©Andreas Hilbeck / pixelio.de

Manufactured and distributed by brebook publishing software
(www.brebook.com)

Walter Jerrold

Oliver Wendell Holmes by Walter Jerrold

OLIVER WENDELL HOLMES

BY

WALTER JERROLD

With a Portrait

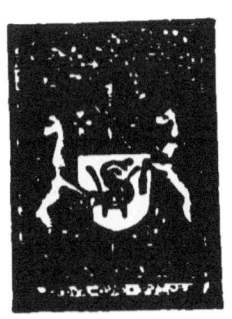

LONDON:

SWAN SONNENSCHEIN AND CO.

NEW YORK: MACMILLAN AND CO

1893.

CONTENTS.

OLIVER WENDELL HOLMES.

I.

THE MAN.

" There's Holmes, who is matchless among you for wit;
A Leyden-jar always full-charged, from which flit
The electrical tingles of hit after hit;
In long poems 't is painful sometimes, and invites
A thought of the way the new Telegraph writes,
Which pricks down its sharp little sentences spitefully
As if you got more than you'd title to rightfully,
And you find yourself hoping its wild father Lightning
Would flame in for a second and give you a fright'ning.
He has perfect sway of what *I* call a sham metre,
But many admire it, the English pentameter,
And Campbell, I think, wrote most commonly worse,
With less nerve, swing, and fire in the same kind of verse,
Nor e'er achieved aught in 't so worthy of praise
As the tribute of Holmes to the grand *Marseillaise.*
You went crazy last year over Bulwer's *New Timon;—*
Why, if B., to the day of his dying, should rhyme on,
Heaping verses on verses and tomes upon tomes,
He could ne'er reach the best point and vigor of Holmes.
His are just the fine hands, too, to weave you a lyric
Full of fancy, fun, feeling, or spiced with satiric,

I

In a measure so kindly, you doubt if the toes
That are trodden upon are your own or your foes'."

            LOWELL.—*A Fable for Critics.*

OLIVER WENDELL HOLMES was born on
   August 29th, 1809, in the historic town—" we
called it then a village "—of Cambridge, Massachusetts. Cambridge then differed very widely
from what it is to-day;[1] Lowell, ten years the
junior of Holmes, has described in his *Fireside
Travels*[2] the Cambridge of his boyhood; and from
his descriptions we can easily conjure up a picture
of the " country village, with its own habits and
traditions," yet with " some of that cloistered quiet
which characterises all university towns." Let
those who are greatly interested in the early life
of Oliver Wendell Holmes turn to the first pages
of *The Poet at the Breakfast Table* and there re-
read the beautiful story of the " Gambrel-roofed
House "—" my birthplace, the home of my childhood, and earlier and later boyhood."

   The father of Oliver Wendell was the Reverend
Abdiel Holmes, pastor of the first Congregational
Church in Cambridge, who had entered into the
gambrel-roofed house two years before the birth
of his third child and first son in the *annus*

---

   [1] Its population, which was then under 4000, in 1880
was upwards of 52,000.
   [2] *Literary Essays*, vol. i. collected edition of his works.

mirabilis of the nineteenth century.[1] The poet's grandfather, Doctor David Holmes, had served in the French and Indian wars and as a surgeon in the American army during the struggle for independence ; *his* grandfather was one of the original settlers of Woodstock county, and was descended from Thomas Holmes, a lawyer of Gray's Inn, London. Holmes's mother was a daughter of Oliver Wendell, a lawyer, of Dutch descent,[2] and was connected with the intellectual aristocracy of New England—the Wendells, the Olivers, the Quinceys, and the Bradstreets. The last-named family included Anne Dudley Bradstreet, who

---

[1] 1809 was also the birth year of Darwin, Gladstone, Tennyson, and Lincoln.

[2] In *Post Prandial*, a poem read before the Phi Beta Kappa Society in 1881, "Wendell Phillips, orator, and Charles Godfrey Leland, poet," being the two men specially honoured, Holmes said—

" ' The Dutch have taken Holland,'—so the schoolboys used
    to say ;
The Dutch have taken Harvard,—no doubt of that to-day !
For the Wendells were low Dutchmen, and all their vrows
    were Vans ;
And the Breitmanns are high Dutchmen, and here is
    honest Hans.
Mynheers, you both are welcome ! Fair cousin Wendell P.,
Our ancestors were dwellers beside the Zuyder Zee ;
Both Grotius and Erasmus were countrymen of we,
And Vondel was our namesake, though he spelt it with
    a V."—*Poems*, iii. 155-6.

occupies in her country's annals the proud position
of being its first poet.   Her poems were published
in London, in 1650, under the quaint title of *The
Tenth Muse, lately Sprung up in America*, a work
now known but to few other than students of
American literature.   The volume has, however,
some nervous, stirring lines in it among much that
certainly would affect us little to-day, except to
move us to smile at the occasional quaintness.   A
couple of lines from *A Dialogue between Old England and New* will sufficiently indicate the class of
poetry to which Anne Bradstreet's work belongs—

> "Farewell, dear mother, Parliament prevail,
>   And in a while you'll tell another tale."

The "Tenth Muse" is of course chiefly interesting
at this date as having been the great-great-grand-
mother of Oliver Wendell Holmes's grandmother.
One of her poems is worthy of more than passing
note, for it appears to indicate a blood-connection
between the poet-subject of this small volume and
the poet-hero of Zutphen; the poem is *An Elegie
on Sir Philip Sidney*, and contains this couplet—

> "Let then, none disallow of these my straines,
>   Which have the selfsame blood yet in my veines."

In the study of the old gambrel-roofed house
and in a certain book-closet on which the Autocrat descants, young Holmes early browsed among
books of all kinds, and imbibed a taste for them—
not only the taste of the reader but that of the

bibliophile also, as is obvious in many parts of his writings. We have, indeed, several references more or less direct to the poet's early life and its surroundings, sometimes fully as in the essay on his birthplace already referred to, and in a beautiful description of the old garden which occurs in some papers on *The Seasons*[1] published in *The Atlantic Almanac* in 1868; often as slight references which are none the less useful as true autobiographic touches.

His early education Oliver received at dames' schools. Mrs. Prentiss was the name of his second schoolmistress, and she appears to have been a good, kindly old soul, who ruled her flock of youngsters with a long willow rod which reached quite across the schoolroom—"reminding, rather than chastening," as her young pupil later described it. Having attained the mature age of ten Holmes was removed from the care of Dame Prentiss and sent to the Cambridgeport School, where he remained for about five years, and where he numbered among his schoolmates Margaret Fuller and Richard Henry Dana, junior. The next educational advance was to Phillips's Academy, Andover, whither Holmes went at the age of fifteen—a vivacious, bright, sensitive and imaginative boy—to prepare himself for the yet more advanced stage of college life. His boyish character at this time he

---

[1] Included in vol. viii. of the collected works.

has himself summed up as "moderately studious, fond of reading stories (even in school hours), also of whispering and whittling his desk." And again he says:—"Exceptional boys of fourteen or fifteen make home a heaven it is true; but I have suspected late in life that I was not one of the exceptional kind. I had tendencies in the direction of flageolets and octave flutes. I had a pistol and a gun and popped at everything that stirred, pretty nearly, except the house-cat. Worse than this, I would buy a cigar and smoke it by instalments, putting it meantime in the barrel of my pistol, by a stroke of ingenuity which it gives me a grim pleasure to recall, for no maternal or other female eyes would explore the cavity of that dread implement in search of contraband commodities."

From all which we may gather that he was a regular boyish boy. While at Andover the youth first attempted poetry—though not in the direction in which he was destined to distinguish himself—by translating the first book of the _Æneid_ into heroic couplets; the result of this bold flight may be read at the end of the last volume of Holmes's collected poems.

Directly after leaving the Andover Academy— he stayed there but for one year—young Holmes entered, in 1825, at Harvard, where he soon became a popular member of several of the college clubs and societies. His talents as versifier were at once noted and made of use, and he was chosen for the proud position of "class poet." At college he made many friends, for although studious he was no "mere bookworm," and was always ready to join in the general round of youthful amusement and pleasantry.

In 1827, when the first regular art exhibition at Boston was opened, Holmes and a couple of his young college friends—John Osborne Sargent and Park Benjamin—produced a small volume of *Poetical Illustrations of the Athenæum Gallery of Paintings*; the verses being, as one might imagine from the authors' youthfulness, mainly satirical. A few years later the same trio united in writing a gift-book, *The Harbinger*, the profits from which were given to some charity. Holmes was one of the members of his class distinguished by election into the Phi Beta Kappa Society. During his life at Harvard, Holmes contributed various poems to the college periodicals,[1] and delivered others before the members of the clubs or societies to which he belonged or was invited. In 1829 he graduated. For a year afterwards he studied law, but then gave it up, determined to follow the doctor's rather than the lawyer's profession.

---

[1] To *The Collegian*, for instance, he contributed some very characteristic humorous pieces ; among others— *The Height of the Ridiculous ; Evening : by a Tailor ;* and *he Spectre Pig.*

In 1830, "with a pencil in the White Chamber *stans pede in uno* pretty nearly," Oliver Wendell Holmes wrote *Old Ironsides*, a lyrical protest against the breaking up of the old frigate *Constitution*. It was published in the *Boston Daily Advertiser* two days after the author had read the paragraph which inspired it. The verses were extensively copied in newspapers all over the country, were even printed on handbills and circulated in the streets—the frigate was saved from the hands of the destroyer and the young poet tasted of fame.

Having wisely decided upon medicine as a pursuit more congenial than the law, Holmes immediately commenced his studies, which he pursued for over two years at home, and then, in 1833, went to Europe, where, after doing the "grand tour," he settled down to work in the hospitals and lecture-rooms of Paris and Edinburgh. Much pleasant reminiscence of this first visit to Europe is contained in the volume—*Our Hundred Days in Europe*—which he wrote when, half a century later, he again crossed the Atlantic. In 1836, he returned to Harvard and took his degree as Doctor of Medicine. On his return, too, he read to the members of the Phi Beta Kappa Society, his *Poetry: A Metrical Essay*; a poem which, in his own words, "presents the simple and partial views of a young person trained after the school of classical English verse as represented by Pope,

Goldsmith and Campbell, with whose lines his memory was early stocked." How much more it "presents" we shall more fitly consider when dealing with Holmes as the poet. One who listened to the delivery of this poem thus recorded his impression of the speaker :—" Extremely youthful in appearance, bubbling over with the mingled humour and pathos that have always marked his poetry, and sparkling with the coruscations of his peculiar genius, he delivered the poem with a clear ringing enunciation which imparted to his hearers his own enjoyment of his thoughts and expressions."

It was in this same year, 1836, too, that Holmes published his first collection of poems, a small volume, of which the *pièce* was the metrical essay *Poetry*, but which also included some of the writer's most eminently characteristic humorous verses. The poet was not, however, cultivating the muse at the expense of the profession which he had adopted, as is sufficiently well evidenced by the fact that during the two years 1836–7, of four medals which were offered for medical dissertations, Doctor Holmes succeeded in carrying off three. The essays which gained him these honours were published in 1838.

In 1837 Holmes's father, the Reverend Abdiel Holmes,—" that most delightful of sunny old men " —died at the age of seventy.

After he had been practising for about a couple

of years in Boston, Doctor Holmes received an appointment as Professor of Anatomy and Physiology at Dartmouth College. This, however, he resigned on his marriage two years later, and returned once more to his well-loved Boston, where he recommenced practice as physician. He married—June 16th, 1840—Amelia Lee Jackson, daughter of Judge Jackson of the Supreme Court of Massachusetts. This second term of practice was not however very long continued; for a few years later, in 1847, he was appointed Parkman Professor of Anatomy and Physiology in the Medical School of Harvard; in which capacity, for a long series of years (he resigned in 1882), Professor Holmes was in the habit of delivering four lectures during each week of the eight months that form the academic year.

When Charles Dickens went to America in 1842, he was fêted at Boston as at all other places which he visited; a grand dinner was given in his honour, and Holmes wrote an extremely graceful song[1] of welcome for the occasion. The following year the popular doctor delivered before the Phi Beta Kappa Society one of his long poems entitled *An After Dinner Poem* (*Terpsichore*).[2] More particular reference to these and similar works which it is necessary to mention in this

---

[1] *Poems*, i. 81.   [2] *Poems*, i. 134.

chronological arrangement will be made in the next section of this book when I come to consider Oliver Wendell Holmes the Poet. In 1846 *A Rhymed Lesson (Urania)* [1] was read before the Boston Mercantile Library Association. In 1851, at the annual gathering of the members of the class of 1829, the first of Holmes's long series of delightful poems, which in his collected works are grouped as *Poems of the Class of* 1829, was delivered; since then but very rarely was a year missed by the poet in celebrating in fitting verse each time-thinned gathering of his college contemporaries.

In 1852 Holmes commenced as a Lyceum lecturer, delivering what must have been, from him, an extremely interesting course on *English Poets of the Nineteenth Century*, concluding each lecture, characteristically enough, with a poem on the poet of whom he had been treating. The lectures have never been published, so far as I am aware, but the peroration poems are included in the collected edition of his works. [2] The style of these lectures was described by one who listened to them as " precise and animated; the illustrations sharp and clearly cut. In the criticism there was a leaning rather to the bold and dashing bravura of Scott and Byron than to the calm philosophical mood of Wordsworth. Where there was any game on the

---

[1] *Poems*, i. 107.　　　[2] *Ibid*, i. 220-229.

wing, when the 'servile herd' of imitators and poetasters came in view, they were dropped at once by a felicitous shot."

For seven years from 1849—as he describes in the *Autocrat*—Professor Holmes was wont to spend the summer months in a house on the corner of a large estate, which his great-grandfather had bought a century earlier, among the Berkshire hills—" the Switzerland of New England." Here, at Canoe Place,[1] Pittsfield, Holmes had as valued neighbours Nathaniel Hawthorne, Herman Melville, G. P. R. James, and other literary notabilities. Thus, in the exercise of two professions, in each of which he was a master, in the city which he loved—" the hub of the solar system "[2] he nicknamed its chief building—the much-loved friend and teacher of a wide circle of his countrymen, the poet and humourist, widely appreciated by all English-speaking people, passed the uneventful life of a literary man.

The year 1857 is a very significant one in the life-story of Oliver Wendell Holmes as a man of letters. In the November of that year there was started, in Boston, a new periodical under the editorship of James Russell Lowell, who was supported by an able staff of contributors, both

---

[1] So named by Holmes because of the mark, a canoe, with which the Indian sachem had signed away the land.

[2] *Autocrat*, p. 125.

American and British—indeed the very first article in the first number was by a British writer on a British man of letters then recently deceased.[1] In accepting the editorship of the new venture Lowell stipulated that Holmes should be one of his principal contributors, and it was Holmes who supplied the title—*The Atlantic Monthly Magazine*. In the first number there appeared an article entitled *The Autocrat of the Breakfast-Table*, which began with strange abruptness, thus : " I was just going to say, when I was interrupted, that one way of classifying minds," etc.[2] This was the first of that triple series of articles which have carried the name which represents the Autocrat, the Professor and the Poet into millions of homes. To those of us who have grown to know and love him from our earliest reading days it is, indeed, difficult to realise that the writer of these books was nearly half a century old when he began them ; that, though acknowledged as a leading Doctor and Professor and as an inimitable writer of " occasional " poetry, he had not struck out what is a line peculiarly his own and had written none of the three remarkable

---

[1] The writer was James Hannay (of *Singleton Fontenoy* fame), and the subject of his essay was Douglas Jerrold, who had died in the previous June.

[2] Holmes had contributed two papers under the same title to an ephemeral periodical during 1832, so that the " interruption " had only lasted for a quarter of a century.

novels which we always associate with his name. The author was, then, close upon fifty years of age before he made any considerable mark upon the literature of his time. The paper in the *Atlantic Monthly* was at once assured of success, and the succeeding numbers of the magazine in which the Autocrat, and, immediately after him, the Professor, monopolised the talk of the breakfast-table were looked for eagerly by large numbers of readers; the poetry the humour, the genial satire,—all were irresistible.

Towards the close of 1859—to be as exact as the author himself, " in the third week of December "— the author of the *Autocrat* appeared before the readers of the *Atlantic Monthly* in an entirely new *rôle*—that of novelist. There then commenced in the pages of the magazine the serial publication of *The Professor's Story*, afterwards republished in volume form under the title of *Elsie Venner : a Romance of Destiny*. The story, despite its subtleties and unconventionalities, was a distinct success, and Oliver Wendell Holmes added the novelist's laurels to those which he already wore in virtu of his success as Doctor, Scientist, Poet and Essayist.

It is curious how, in speaking of each man of letters with whom we become really intimate through his books, we always attach an adjective-label,—" holy " George Herbert, " judicious " Hooker, " quaint old " Izaak Walton (always a double allowance of adjective to the author of the *Compleat Angler*), "gentle" Elia ; with Holmes, the adjective that always unbidden rises to our lips is "genial" ; and geniality is indeed a characteristic of him no less as a writer than as a man ; nay, even as satirist his geniality does not desert him. The homes of the genial Autocrat in Boston were ever places where friends of light and leading were wont to congregate. Many visitors have placed on record the poet's kindness and thoughtfulness to and for all his visitors, whether they be his illustrious friends, like Motley—a frequent and welcome guest—or the latest caller who thinks his great admiration for the writings sufficient warranty for boring the writer. "He is the perfect essence of wit and hospitality," wrote one visitor, "courteous, amiable and entertaining to a degree, which is more easily remembered than imparted or described. If the caller expects to find blue-blood snobbishness at 296, Beacon Street,[1] he will be disappointed. It is one of the most elegant and charming residences on that broad and fashionable thoroughfare, but far less pre-tentious, both inwardly and outwardly, than many of the others. . . . The chief point of attraction,

---

[1] Holmes's third Boston residence after his marriage in 1840. After living for eighteen years at 8, Montgomery Place, Holmes spent twelve at 164, Charles Street, and from there moved to Beacon Street.

for the visitor as well as the host, is in the magnificent and spacious library, which may be more aptly termed the Autocrat's workshop."

From the library-window of this house an extended view is obtained over the river Charles, and a wide expanse of town and country, including a glimpse of the poet's distant birthplace,—

"Through my north window, in the wintry weather,—
  My airy oriel on the river shore,—
I watch the sea-fowl as they flock together
  Where late the boatman flashed his dripping oar." [1]

A visitor describing the same room and its view says : " The ancient Hebrew always had a window open towards Jerusalem, the city about which his most cherished hopes and memories clustered, and this window gives its owner the pleasure of looking straight to the place of his birth, and thus of freshening all the happy memories of a successful life." [2]   The library must indeed be an interesting place, not to lovers of the poet alone but also to the bibliophile—who it is to be hoped is no less a lover of the poet, he should be rather more, for Doctor Holmes is an eloquent enthusiast on the subject of his book rarities. This may be seen at once in many passages scattered up and down the *Breakfast-Table Series*, passages reminiscent not only of the volumes themselves but of the par-

---

[1] " My Aviary," *Poems*, iii. 66.
[2] Arthur Gilman, *Poets' Homes*, second series, p. 21.

ticular circumstances in which they were read or acquired. One old leather-bound *Tulpius*, for instance, was, Holmes says, "my only reading when in quarantine at Marseilles," another "find" had "strayed in among the rubbish of the bookstall on the boulevard."

Like other men of mark Doctor Holmes has often been troubled by autograph seekers, by impertinent visitors and would-be authors, anxious to obtain his opinion on their work, and his fame as the "genial" Holmes has, we may be sure, not tended to decrease the number of his tormentors. For the guidance of authors similarly circumstanced, he drew up a humorous code of rules which they might follow. It does of course at times happen that in the ranks of the aspiring writers who send specimens of their work to be judged may be men of distinct promise ; often it is probable they get dismissed with "the ruck," though not invariably so, for on one occasion a young Californian writer sent a sample of his poetry and asked Holmes whether he considered it worth while the writer continuing. Holmes was evidently in this case impressed by the promising originality shown, and wrote the wished-for letter of encouragement. Some time had passed and he thought no more of his Californian correspondent, when a gentleman called and asked if he remembered the incident. "I do, indeed,"

2

replied Holmes. " Well," remarked his visitor, " I
am the man."   It proved to be Bret Harte.

In 1862, the poems which the author had written
since 1849 were published together in a volume
entitled *Songs in Many Keys*, which included the
beautiful ballad of *Agnes* and many other poems
familiar to the lovers of Holmes.   On August 19th
of the same year the poet's mother died upwards of
ninety years old—" a bright, keen-witted, vivacious
woman, much beloved by her neighbours and by
her husband's parishioners."

During the war of attempted secession Holmes's
elder son—who bears his father's name—was twice
wounded in battle, once—at Antietam, September
16th, 1862—somewhat seriously.   In a delightful
paper contributed to the *Atlantic Monthly*, entitled
My Hunt after the Captain,[1] Oliver Wendell
Holmes " the elder " gives a graphic account of his
journey to the front, and back, and then forward
again, on an anxious, and for some time fruitless,
hunt for his son.   On Independence Day of the
following year (July 4th, 1863), Holmes delivered
an oration before the city authorities of Boston.
This oration—*The Inevitable Trial*[2]—was a magnificent, stirring call to his countrymen to be true
to themselves and to liberty—to continue the war,
if need were, to the bitter end, even though that

---

[1] *Pages from an Old Volume of Life*, p. 16.
[2] *Pages from an Old Volume of Life*, p. 78.

end were to be annihilation—better annihilation, than compromise with wrong. Stirring reading as *The Inevitable Trial* forms now, when the war-scars are a generation old, and to persons knowing of the great struggle but by hearsay and history, it must have sounded in the ears of the orator's fellow-townsmen, in the mid-period of the greatly significant war, with the ringing notes of a bugle-call to action. It forms by no means an oration of only temporary value and interest, which ceased immediately upon the triumph of the cause in which it was spoken, but it is a piece of sterling, virile literature.

In 1866, Holmes collected several of his miscellaneous writings and published them as *Soundings from the Atlantic.* Some of the papers in this volume are included in *Pages from an Old Volume of Life*, but some of them have not been reprinted, and among these there is a very amusing supposed interview between a Reporter and the Autocrat's landlady, and *A Visit to the Asylum for Decayed Punsters* which is far from being in Holmes's happiest vein. The first named of these two papers, however, is a piece of characteristic writing, giving the landlady's views of the Autocrat and the "Schoolma'am." "This gentleman" (the landlady is made to say) "warn't no great of a gentleman to look at. Being of a very moderate dimension—five foot five, he said, but five foot four

more likely, and I've heerd him say he didn't
weigh much over a hundred and twenty pound.
He was light complected rather than darksome,
and was one of them smooth-faced people that
keep their baird and wiskers cut close, jest as if
they'd be very troublesome if they let 'em grow,—
instead of layin' out their face in grass, as my poor
husband that's dead and gone used to say.   He
was a well-behaved gentleman at table, only talked
a good deal, and pretty loud sometimes, and had
a way of turnin' up his nose when he didn't like
what folks said, that one of my boarders, who is
a very smart young man, said he couldn't stand,
no how, and used to make faces and poke fun
at him, whenever he see him do it. . . . Many's
the time I've seen that gentleman keepin' two or
three of 'em sittin' round the breakfast-table after
the rest had swallowed their meal and the things
was cleared off and Bridget was a-waitin' to get
the cloth away,—and there that little man would
set with a tumbler of sugar and water,—what he
used to call O Sukray,—a-talkin' and a-talkin',—
and sometimes he would laugh, and sometimes
the tears would come into his eyes,—which was a
kind of grayish blue eyes,—and there he'd set and
set, and my boy Benjamin Franklin hangin' round
and gettin' late for school and wantin' an excuse,
and an old gentleman that's one of my boarders,
a-listenin' as if he wa'n't no older than my

Ben Franklin, and that schoolmistress settin'
jest as if she'd been bewitched, and you might
stick pins into her without her hollerin'. He was
a master hand to talk when he got a-goin'. . . . .
One of my boarders used to say that he always
said exactly what he was a mind to, and stuck his
idees out jest like them that sells pears outside
their shop-winders,—some is three cents, some is
two cents, and some is only one cent, and if you
don't like, you needn't buy, but them's the articles
and them's the prices, and if you want 'em, take
'em, and if you don't, go about your business, and
don't stand mellerin' of 'em with your thumbs all
day till you've sp'ilt 'em for other folks." [1]

This humorous description of himself is delightful, as is the whole paper from which it is quoted.
It seems a pity that the Autocrat has not seen fit
to include it in the collected edition of his works,
for it would form a most appropriate foreword or
afterword to the *Breakfast-Table Series*. As a
pendant to this description of himself as seen
through his landlady's eyes we may notice the
following passage, which describes him as he
appeared to a Scotchman who heard him as medical
lecturer during the sixties. "Holmes is a plain,
little dapper man, his short hair brushed down
like a boy's, but turning grey now; a trifle of

---

[1] *Soundings from the Atlantic:* Boston, 1866, p. 334,
et seq.

furzy hair under his ears ; a powerful jaw, and a
thick, strong underlip that gives decision to his
look, with a dash of pertness. In conversation, he
is animated and cordial—sharp, too, taking the
word out of one's mouth." [1]

In 1867 *The Guardian Angel,* which had run
through the *Atlantic Monthly* in serial form, was
published. At the close of the same year, under
the part editorship of Holmes, was issued *The
Atlantic Almanac,* which is especially interesting
as being the medium through which the quadruple essay of *The Seasons* [2] was first published.
This essay, or set of essays, not only gives us
exquisite bits of prose descriptive of nature in New
England, but is also valuable and attractive on
account of the gems of reminiscence included in it
—some particularly beautiful passages descriptive
of the old garden of the gambrel-roofed house, and of
the " September gale of 1815." [3] " I embalmed some
of my fresher recollections of it in a copy of verses
which some of my readers may have seen. I am
afraid there is something of what we may call,
indulgently, negative veracity in that youthful
effusion." And of the celebration of " commencement " at Cambridge in the writer's boyhood,—
" In the last week of August used to fall Com-

---

[1] David Macrae, *The Americans at Home,* ii., p. 243.
[2] *Pages from an Old Volume of Life,* p. 132.
[3] See also *Poems,* i., p. 29.

mencement day at Cambridge. I remember that
week well, for something happened to me once at
that time, namely, I was born." [1]

In June 1870 Dr. Holmes delivered a thoughtful
and valuable address on the subject of *Mechanism
in Thought and Morals* [2] before the members of the
Phi Beta Kappa Society; to this paper we shall
refer more fully in a later section. In the
following year the breakfast-table speaker tried
a dangerous experiment—an experiment which
success alone could justify. It was over ten years
since the Professor had kissed an unseen farewell
to his breakfast-table companions after occupying
for twelve months the chair from which his friend
the Autocrat had delightfully dogmatised; yet
Holmes placed the Poet at the *Atlantic* " breakfast-
table," and completed what have since come to be
looked upon as an inseparable trinity,—the " three
starveling volumes bound in one " of his own
Epilogue.

In 1878 Holmes performed a painful task,
although a labour of love, in writing the biography
of a fellow-collegian and lifelong friend who had
earned a world-wide reputation as historian. This
friend was J. L. Motley, and the volume which
tells the story of his life is interesting alike from
its subject and its author. It must however be

---

[1] *Pages from an Old Volume of Life*, p. 158.
[2] *Ibid.*, p. 260.

confessed that Holmes is far from being at his best in such a set task as the writing of a man's life must necessarily be.

In 1879 the publishers of the *Atlantic Monthly* determined to celebrate the seventieth birthday of their invaluable supporter—his " Sabbath decade " as he happily termed it—by a grand breakfast which was duly given on December 3rd,[1] that date being a more generally convenient one than the true anniversary (August 29th). At this breakfast most of the leading luminaries of American literature gathered together to do honour to Holmes —Emerson, Whittier and Harriet Beecher Stowe were among the veterans there, while the younger generation of writers was well represented. The guest of the occasion read a characteristic and deeply moving poem, entitled *The Iron Gate*,[2] concluding with " Thanks, brothers, sisters,— children,—and farewell," as though his work was finished.   Four out of the thirteen volumes which form his collected works had yet to be written, and besides he was destined yet to write—in years all

---

[1] Miss E. E. Brown, in her *Life of Holmes*, says that it took place on the " thirteenth of November "; Mr. Kennedy, in his *Life*, gives it correctly and explicitly, thus, "the third day of December from one and a half to four o'clock n the afternoon."

[2] *Poems*, iii., p. 56, and quoted at the conclusion of this volume.

too few—the biography of the greatest of those who were gathered together to do him honour—Ralph Waldo' Emerson, and, happily, destined to see his son—Oliver Wendell Holmes the younger, —made a judge of the Supreme Court.

In 1882—after having regularly fulfilled the duties of the appointment for five-and-thirty years —Holmes resigned his Parkman Professorship at Harvard, and was immediately appointed Emeritus Professor of the college. On the twenty-eighth of November he delivered his farewell lecture to his anatomy students ; a storm of applause greeted his arrival; immediately it died away, one of the members of the class came forward and presented, on behalf of all the students, a beautiful loving-cup, bearing engraved upon it, this line from Holmes's own writings—

" Love bless thee, joy crown thee, God speed thy career."

This graceful token of loving admiration so deeply affected the retiring Professor, that, as he wrote in acknowledging the gift by letter, it made him speechless, adding, however, that he was quite sure that they did not mistake *aphasia* for *acardia* —his heart was in its right place though his tongue forgot its office. The following spring the medical profession of New York gave a complimentary dinner to the Doctor, who, in reading a poem to his hosts, asked them to—

"Deal with him as a truant, if you will,
But claim him, keep him, call him brother still."

In 1881 the greatest thinker, the greatest *littérateur* that America has seen, passed away in the person of Ralph Waldo Emerson, known and appreciated throughout the English-speaking world. Dr. Holmes was asked to undertake the writing of a biography of the great Concord sage for the *American Men of Letters* series; this he did, and in 1884 the volume was published. As in his earlier volume of biography the *Life of Emerson*, although extremely interesting, yet it does not strike us as being particularly successful. The author is too much cramped by limitations as to subject and space—for half-a-century he had been writing as he chose on self-chosen subjects, and the change was too great to be unusually successful. The volume is, however, extremely useful, and neither admirers of the Concord philosopher nor of the Autocrat can afford to overlook it. Nearly each year was to show how prematurely Holmes had uttered his "Farewell": in 1885, the year following the publication of the *Life of Emerson*, the third of the Autocrat's novels—*A Mortal Antipathy*—was issued.

In 1886, after fifty years' interval, Doctor Holmes paid a visit to Europe, accompanied by his daughter. He was received everywhere with a delighted welcome—London, Oxford and Cambridge vied with one another in seeing which could do most honour to him during his short stay. Short the stay was, for he remained but little over three months. On his return home he prepared from his diary, with reminiscences of his earlier visit, a book of most delightful gossip which was published in 1887, as *Our Hundred Days in Europe*; a book which will probably maintain popularity as long as the best of Holmes's work ; not, be it understood, that I rank it with the best, but it possesses that charm which belongs to other frankly egoistic books, and in virtue of which they continue to be read. It treats largely of notable persons and places "flourishing" during the eighties ; and this, given in the friendly, familiar, *personal* style of Oliver Wendell Holmes, gives the book just that power of fascination, which is, perhaps, even a greater passport to posterity than is greatness itself. Of his account of the *Hundred Days*, Holmes himself says : " My reader was fairly forewarned that this narrative was to be more like a chapter of autobiography than the record of a tourist. In the language of philosophy, it is written from a subjective, not an objective, point of view. It is not exactly a ' Sentimental Journey,' though there are warm passages here and there which end with notes of admiration. I remind myself now and then of certain other travellers : of Benjamin of Tudela, going from the hospitalities

of one son of Abraham to another; of John
Buncle, finding the loveliest of women under every
roof that sheltered him; sometimes, perhaps, of
that tipsy rhymester [1] whose record of his good
and bad fortunes at the hands of landlords and
landladies is enlivened by an occasional touch of
humour, which makes it palatable to coarse literary
feeders. But in truth these papers have many
of the characteristics of private letters written
home to friends. They *are* written for friends,
rather than for a public which cares nothing
about the writer. I knew there were many such
whom it would please to know where the writer
went, whom he saw and what he saw, and how
he was impressed by persons and things." [2]

In a recent letter to the writer, dated September
18th, 1893, Dr. Holmes says: " I send you one of
my printed formulæ to show you how hard I treat
my correspondents." The enclosure is a printed
card, in which the venerable author says that it is
impossible for him to do more than acknowledge
the numerous communications from near and
distant friends, finding his time, his eyes, and his
hand overtaxed by an increasing correspondence.
Not to disappoint his correspondents, however, the
genial old man signs the "printed formulæ."

---

[1] *Drunken Barnabee.*
[2] *Our Hundred Days in Europe,* p. 183.

II.

THE POET.

THE CHIEFTAIN, BY WILLIAM WINTER.[1]

*Read at the " Atlantic " Festival, in Commemoration of the
Seventieth Birthday of Oliver Wendell Holmes, at
Boston, December 3, 1879.*

If that glad song had ebbed away,
   Which, rippling on through smiles and tears,
Has bathed with showers of diamond spray
   The rosy fields of seventy years,—
If that sweet voice were hushed to-day,
     What should we say ?

At first we thought him but a jest
   A ray of laughter, quick to fade ;
We did not dream how richly blest
   In his pure life our lives were made :
Till soon the aureole shone, confest,
     Upon his crest.

When violets fade the roses blow ;
   When laughter dies the passions wake :
His royal song that slept below,
   Like Arthur's sword beneath the lake,
Long since has flashed its fiery glow
     O'er all we know.

---

[1] *The Poems of William Winter*: Boston, 1881, p. 151.

That song has poured its sacred light
  On crimson flags in freedom's van,
And blessed their serried ranks, who fight
  Life's battle here for truth and man—
An oriflamme, to cheer the right,
      Through darkest night !

That song has flecked with rosy gold
  The sails that fade o'er fancy's sea ;
Relumed the storied days of old ;
  Presaged the glorious life to be ;
And many a sorrowing heart consoled
      In grief untold.

When, shattered on the loftiest steep
  The statesman's glory ever found,
That heart, so like the boundless deep,
  Broke, in the deep no heart can bound,
How did his dirge of sorrow weep
      O'er Webster's sleep !

How sweetly did his spirit pour
  The strains that make the tear-drops start,
When, on this bleak New England shore,
  With Tara's harp and Erin's heart,
He thrilled us to the bosom's core
      With thoughts of Moore !

The shamrock, green on Liffey's side,
  The lichen 'neath New England snows,
White daisies of the fields of Clyde,
  Twined ardent round old Albion's rose,
Bloom in his verse, as blooms the bride
      With love and pride.

The silken tress, the mantling wine,
  Red roses, summer's whispering leaves,

The lips that kiss, the hands that twine,
  The heart that loves, the heart that grieves—
They all have found a deathless shrine
    In his rich line!

Ah well, that voice can charm us yet,
  And still that shining tide of song,
Beneath a sun not soon to set,
  In golden music flows along.
With dew of joy our eyes are wet—
    Not of regret.

For still, as comes the festal day,
  In many a temple, far and near,
The words that all have longed to say,
  The words that all are proud to hear,
Fall from his lips, with conquering sway,
    Or grave or gay.

No moment this for passion's heat,
  Nor mine the voice to give it scope,
When love and fame and beauty meet
  To crown their Memory and their Hope!
I cast white lilies, cool and sweet,
    Here at his feet.

True bard, true soul, true man, true friend!
  Ah, gently on that reverend head
Ye snows of wintry age descend,
  Ye shades of mortal night be shed!
Peace guide and guard him to the end,
    And God defend!

THERE is a rare pathetic touch about some of
Holmes's unique *vers d'occasion* which, probably entirely overlooked at the time of the verses
being spoken, is not too obvious even to those
reading the poet in their study. It is found

where the poet explains how well he is aware that
all his listeners have come ready to smile at the
anticipated "funny things," to pucker their lips
at his first pun, and to roar with laughter at the
coming *mot*—

> "I know my audience. All the gay and young
> Love the light antics of a playful tongue;
> And these, remembering some expansive line
> My lips let loose among the nuts and wine,
> Are all impatience till the opening pun
> Proclaims the witty shamfight is begun.
> Two-fifths at least, if not the total half,
> Have come infuriate for an earthquake laugh.
>
>   *   *   *   *   *
>
> "I know a tailor, once a friend of mine,
> Expects great doings in the button line,—
> For mirth's concussions rip the outward case,
> And plant the stitches in a tenderer place.
> I know my audience,—these shall have their due;
> A smile awaits them ere my song is through!"[1]

They have come, that is, to be amused and
tickled by the humorist and wit rather than to
be elevated and edified by the poet and philosopher.
Yet though the poet recognises this, and in his
quiet, half-playful, half-reproving way thus tells
his audience that he does so, he manages to give
them much wisdom and much beautiful poetry,
along with the quaintness of expression and illus-

---

[1] *Poems*, i., p. 108.

tration—the verbal quips and cranks which had come to be looked upon as the most important of his literary merchandise, and the rightful due of those who listened to him. This character for pleasantry which he had so early acquired—*Urania*, from which the above passage is quoted, was written in 1846—has probably been largely responsible for the colouring of the whole, or at any rate a great part, of Holmes's poetic work. Even with some of the essentially pathetic pieces, there is yet an atmosphere of humour through which they are seen. Take, for example, from among the earlier poems, *The Last Leaf*, " suggested by the sight of old Major Melville in his cocked hat and breeches," [1] which won the commendation of so fastidious a critic as Edgar Allan Poe, who indeed made a copy of it, which copy fell later into the hands of the gratified author. It was this same poem, too, which so fascinated Abraham Lincoln that he learned it by heart, and was fond of referring to the fourth verse as one of the most pathetic passages in literature :—

> " I saw him once before,
> As he passed by the door,
>   And again
> The pavement stones resound,
> As he totters o'er the ground
>   With his cane.

---

[1] *Mortal Antipathy*, p. 8.

" They say that in his prime,
  Ere the pruning-knife of Time
      Cut him down,
  Not a better man was found
  By the Crier on his round
      Through the town.

" But now he walks the streets,
  And he looks at all he meets
      Sad and wan,
  And he shakes his feeble head,
  That it seems as if he said,
      ' They are gone.'

" The mossy marbles rest
  On the lips that he has prest
      In their bloom,
  And the names he loved to hear
  Have been carved for many a year
      On the tomb.

" My grandmamma has said—
  Poor old lady, she is dead
      Long ago—
  That he had a Roman nose,
  And his cheek was like a rose
      In the snow.

" But now his nose is thin,
  And it rests upon his chin
      Like a staff,
  And a crook is in his back,
  And a melancholy crack
      In his laugh.

" I know it is a sin
  For me to sit and grin
      At him here ;

But the old three-cornered hat,
And the breeches and all that,
Are so queer!

"And if I should live to be
The last leaf upon the tree
In the spring,
Let them smile, as I do now,
At the old forsaken bough
Where I cling."[1]

The second and fifth verses show us the humourist rather over-colouring the work of the poet. "The pruning-knife of Time," for instance, seems to be out of keeping with the quiet pathetic feeling of the greater part of the poem, which is just sufficiently charged with humour to keep it truly pathetic without being sentimental; it is, indeed, a very good example of that close interconnection of humour and pathos which is so often remarked, and to which it is, perhaps, that such writers as Charles Lamb owe their peculiar place in our affections.

The too-pronounced presence of the humourist, although it may jar upon us in reading some of Holmes's pathetic poems, is yet only an occasional blemish; generally the humour is but like the glow of summer lightning, bringing what it illumines nearer to us, while at times the humourist is not present at all—no more than

----

[1] *Poems*, i., p. 3.

the Thomas Hood of *The Epping Hunt* and *The Tale of a Trumpet* is visible in the Thomas Hood of *The Bridge of Sighs* and *The Song of the Shirt*—witness the short, sharp, defiant yet exultant ring of *Old Ironsides*. The fervour of the opening line—

"Ay, tear her tattered ensign down—"[1]

rings through the whole poem, making our pulses leap and our blood tingle as with a sudden blare of trumpet. Small wonder is it that this short impromptu[2] should have echoed and re-echoed throughout the States—serving effectually its object of saving the old frigate *Constitution*, popularly known as *Old Ironsides*, from proposed destruction. In another of these earlier poems also—*The Cambridge Churchyard*—we have a sustained flight of

"The lonely spirit of the mournful lay,
Which lives immortal as the verse of Gray."[3]

How truly Gray-like in both form and spirit, for instance, is this single stanza—a stanza which embodies in itself the *motif* of the whole poem—

"Hast thou a tear for buried love?
A sigh for transient power?
All that a century left above
Go, read it in an hour!"[4]

---

[1] *Poems*, i., p. 2.   [3] *Poems*, i., p. 41.
[2] See *ante*, p. 8.   [4] *Ibid.*, i., p. 6.

It is simple in expression, yet direct in meaning as Goldsmith himself might have written.

In 1851 Mary Russell Mitford devoted a section (xxxi.) of her pleasant *Recollections of a Literary Life* to Oliver Wendell Holmes, and this she did mainly on the strength of one poem, *Astræa*,—" a little book of less than forty pages "—that had been delivered before the Phi Beta Kappa Society the previous year. This instant recognition by Miss Mitford of the poet from over sea is especially noteworthy as taking place before the publication of the first English edition of; Holmes's poems. A year later that first English edition appeared, and probably owed its appearance at that time to the unqualified welcome extended to it by a critic of such true instinct as Mary Russell Mitford. A glance at these words of welcome, in the light of the poet's later great success, may well interest us. In introducing those passages from *Astræa* which had especially attracted her, the critic says : "In these days of curious noyelty, nothing has taken me more pleasantly by surprise than the school of true and original poetry that has sprung up among our blood-relations (I had well-nigh called them our fellow-countrymen) across the Atlantic; they who speak the same tongue and inherit the same literature. And of all this flight of genuine poets, I hardly know any one so original as Dr. Holmes. For him we can find no living prototype; to track his footsteps, we must travel back as far as Pope or Dryden; and, to my mind, it would be well if some of our own bards would take the same journey—provided always it produced the same result. Lofty, poignant, graceful, grand, high of thought and clear of word, we could fancy ourselves reading some pungent page of *Absalom and Achitophel*, or of the *Moral Epistles*, if it were not for the pervading nationality, which, excepting Whittier, American poets have generally wanted,[1] and for that true reflection of the manners and the follies of the age, without which satire would fail alike of its purpose and its name."

Poetry has probably existed as long as human language, yet an adequate definition of what it really is that we mean by the word is yet to seek. It has been attempted numberless times by widely different persons; as often has it been sought, perhaps, as the true meaning of another word— wit. Yet, despite this, we are far from having a satisfactory definition of either of them. Indeed it is probable that when found it will be discovered that it embraces the two. I myself do not intend adding to the number of those who have sought to express in an axiom what poetry exactly is and what it is not, for, as quaint old Isaac Barrow expresses

[1] Whitman's first volume was not issued until four years later; while none of Lowell's "national" poetry had been issued.

it with regard to wit, "often it consisteth in one knows not what, and springeth up one can hardly tell how." All that we can say is, I do not know what poetry is, but *this* is poetry, forthwith giving an example of much riches of thought in a little room of words. To show in Holmes's poetry the simple terseness of expression with which he conveys a deal of meaning, we may take such lines as these on the first approach of spring, where the second half of the first line—in its context—suggests so very much more than the words would ordinarily convey :—

" Doubtful at first, suspected more than seen,
The southern slopes are fringed with tender green." [1]

Or, in another vein, we may take such an example as this—

" Alone, alone, the awful past I tread
White with the marbles of the slumbering dead."

Or this couplet from *Spring*, the same poem from which is taken the first of the two preceding quotations,—a couplet which Miss Mitford instanced as being unmatched in flower painting—

" The spendthrift crocus, bursting through the mould
Naked and shivering with his cup of gold." [2]

Holmes's occasional verse and his more particularly humorous writings we will consider later ;

---

[1] *Poems*, i., p. 197.   [2] *Ibid.*

here we are more especially concerned with his
poetry, which has been—to use a much ill-treated
expression—inspired, that is, written not so much
in accordance with a request from without as in
fulfilment of a command from within. To seek
for such a poet's "models," to say he is of this or
that "school," a follower of this or that "leader,"
a writer in this or the other "mould," were a
difficult task and a thankless. An American
critic,[1] who has exercised his ingenuity on this
question, has found Holmes's chief master, the man
by whom his style was most considerably influenced,
in Thomas Hood ! In support of his criticism,
Mr. Kennedy quotes some verses which he implies,
but does not state, are by Holmes, along with
some stanzas from one of Hood's comic ballads.
The examples given are both in common ballad
metre, but there all similarity ends ; the American
verses do not at all " show to what purpose Hood
was read by Boston and Cambridge people when
Holmes was making his first poems." [2]   Hood's
poems might never have crossed the Atlantic for
any influence of his style discernible in the
Fashionable Eclogue quoted.

> " Next year, papa ! next year, mamma !
>   You know I'm thirty-two,"

is very much more in the style of Thomas Haynes

---

[1] Mr. W. S. Kennedy.
[2] W. S. Kennedy, *O. W. Holmes*, p. 287.

Bayley, or even of Praed, than in that of Hood.
Both Hood and Holmes are true humourists—
both of them have "touched alike the springs of
laughter and the source of tears;"[1] and examples
might, it is true, be quoted, showing the apparent
influence of Hood's punning style—

> "Milton to Stilton would give in, and Solomon to
>   Salmon,
> And Roger Bacon be a bore, and Francis Bacon
>   gammon!"[2]

Or, again, one might take a single poem—*Lexington*,
for instance—and declare that Holmes's poetry bore
distinct evidence of having been influenced by the
songs and melodies of Thomas Moore—

> "Slowly the mist o'er the meadow was creeping,
>   Bright on the dewy buds glistened the sun,
> When from his couch, while his children were sleeping,
>   Rose the bold rebel and shouldered his gun."[3]

Might we not imagine that Erin's laureate himself had touched the harp-strings which responded
thus?   Or, yet again, we might take that exquisite
gem, *The Chambered Nautilus*, and say, Here is the
work of a poet who must have drunk deep and
long at seventeenth-century founts—who is closely
and sympathetically acquainted with Abraham
Cowley, Andrew Marvell, and kindred souls.

---

[1] Douglas Jerrold, dedication of *Cakes and Ale* to Hood.
[2] *Poems*, i. p. 88.   [3] *Ibid.*, i., p. 67.

"This is the ship of pearl, which, poets feign,
    Sails the unshadowed main,—
    The venturous bark that flings
On the sweet summer wind its purpled wings
In gulfs enchanted, where the Siren sings,
    And coral reefs lie bare,
Where the cold sea-maids rise to sun their streaming
    hair." [1]

The task of tracing each line of a poet's work
to some previous writer is, however, an ungracious
one; plagiarism and imitation are less common
than some would have us believe, and what often
appear as such would prove, if proof were possible,
nothing but mere coincidence. "Given certain
factors," as the Autocrat expresses it, "and a
sound brain should always evolve the same fixed
product with the certainty of Babbage's calculating
machine." [2] The youthful poet, with but rarest,
if there be any, exception, will, at first, express
himself in forms with which he is familiar, and the
attainment of a form for himself will be a mere
matter of evolution, as he finds for himself the
way in which it is best for him to give out that
which he has to impart. We might take various
isolated poems or passages from Holmes's works,
showing the apparent influence or imitation of
widely differing writers, as I have shown, yet we
should but little affect his title to originality;

---

[1] *Poems*, ii., p. 107.   [2] *Autocrat*, p. 8.

indeed, early as her criticism was formulated, Miss
Mitford was not far wrong in hailing Holmes as
one of the first of America's peculiarly *national*
poets. He is not national in the sense of having
written for all time the legends of the Indians in
a *Iiawatha*; yet how much more he represents
the peculiar temper of his countrymen than
Longfellow is very obvious on the slightest com-
parison of their works. He is not national in
the sense of having treated of native places and
legends—with their names!—such as we have in
Mogg Megone. Yet there can, I think, be little
doubt about his being even more national than
Whittier, with whom it is that Miss Mitford
brackets him. He is not national in the sense
of having caught and perpetuated in a poem the
dialect of a *Iosea Biglow*; yet I should place him
before Lowell in this regard. He is not national
in the sense of having struck a new vehicle for
poetic expression such as is given us in *The Leaves
of Grass*; yet it is apparent that even more than
Walt Whitman is Holmes peculiarly national.
Longfellow and Lowell, Whittier and Whitman,
each represents some particular phase of the
national life, character, traditions, or peculiarities;
but Holmes draws upon all these, and subtly, yet
consistently, interweaves in his work any such
real difference as may exist between the American
nation and the parent race from which it has

mainly sprung. The result is a curious inter-
weaving of shrewd *Poor Richard*-like common
sense, with high and beautiful thoughts,—the
texture of poetry, which, as I take it, is the most
peculiarly national that America has yet produced. Pegasus has not yet been thoroughly
acclimatised, as yet he is only allowed to fly with
clipped wings, for fear he should fly beyond the
common bound of common sense, or to feel when
he tries a flight that

"The world's cart-collar hugs his throat."[1]

We have, scattered throughout Holmes's three
volumes of poems, delicate hints of stories and traditions of old Colonial days, along with beautiful
descriptive passages, and the constant recurrence of
a mirth-provoking humour often allied with high
moral truths and touching pathos, in a way that
is strikingly characteristic, and which is very much
wanting in what is called, or calls itself, "the new
humour." His many loving references to the old
days before the Declaration of Independence, and
also to "Mother" England, as Mistress Bradstreet
had called it, testify to a certain wholesome con-
servatism in the mind of the poet, and do not one
whit lessen his great love and admiration for the
present Republic. Among his themes, dealing with
the old days in America, not one is more delightful

---

[1] Coventry Patmore : *The Angel in the House.*

than *Dorothy Q., a Family Portrait*, a poem which, written in 1871, has all the freshness and spirit of the author's earlier works, and which is peculiarly representative of his style both of thought and expression.

> " O Damsel Dorothy ! Dorothy Q. !
> Strange is the gift that I owe to you.
>
>   *   *   *   *   *
>
> " What if a hundred years ago
> Those close-shut lips had answered No,
> When forth the tremulous question came
> That cost the maiden her Norman name,
> And under the folds that look so still
> The bodice swelled with the bosom's thrill ?
> Should I be I, or would it be
> One-tenth another, to nine-tenths me ?
>
> " Soft is the breath of a maiden's YES :
> Not the light gossamer stirs with less ;
> But never a cable that holds so fast
> Through all the battles of wave and blast,
> And never an echo of speech or song
> That lives in the babbling air so long !
> There were tones in the voice that whispered then
> You may hear to-day in a hundred men.
>
> " O lady and lover, how faint and far
> Your images hover,—and here we are,
> Solid and stirring in flesh and bone,—
> Edward's and Dorothy's—all their own,—
> A goodly record for Time to show
> Of a syllable spoken so long ago !—
> Shall I bless you, Dorothy, or forgive
> For the tender whisper that bade me live ?

" It shall be a blessing, my little maid !
I will heal the stab of the Red-Coat's blade,
And freshen the gold of the tarnished frame,
And gild with a rhyme your household name." [1]

Dorothy Q. was Dorothy Quincy, Holmes's great-grandmother—

" Grandmother's mother : her age, I guess,
Thirteen summers or something less." [2]

Another delightful story-poem of the old time is
*Grandmother's Story of Bunker-Hill Battle, as she
saw it from the Belfry.* Curiously enough, in this
poem we have at the conclusion a theme similar to
that in the passage just quoted ; after telling her
grandchildren how, as a girl, she had watched the
fight, and fainted, and been carried home—

" When I woke from dreams affrighted the evening lamps
    were lighted,—
On the floor a youth was lying; his bleeding breast was
    bare.

    *   *   *   *   *

" For they all thought he was dying, as they gathered
    round him crying,—
And they said, ' Oh, how they'll miss him ! ' and, ' What
    will his mother do ? '
Then, his eyelids just unclosing like a child's that has
    been dozing,
He faintly murmured, ' Mother ! '—and—I saw his eyes
    were blue.

---

[1] *Poems* ii., p. 206.   [2] *Ibid.*, ii., p. 205.

"'Why, grandma, how you're winking!' Ah, my child,
   it sets me thinking
Of a story not like this one. Well, he somehow lived
   along;
So we came to know each other, and I nursed him like
   a—mother,
Till at last he stood before me, tall, and rosy-cheeked, and
   strong.

"And we sometimes walked together in the pleasant
   summer weather,—
'Please to tell us what his name was?' Just your own,
   my little dear,—
There's his picture Copley painted: we became so well
   acquainted,
That—in short, that's why I'm grandma, and you children
   all are here!"[1]

Another old-world theme is touched upon in
Agnes, which tells, in simple ballad metre and
language, the pathetic story of a New England
knight and his humble love; how he makes her
his mistress and then, she having saved his life
at Lisbon during the earthquake, marries her—

> "Thus Agnes won her noble name,
>   Her lawless lover's hand;
> The lowly maiden so became
>   A lady in the land!"[2]

One of the most striking features of Holmes's
writings—both prose and poetry—is the evidence
of the remarkable power which he has of seizing
upon happy similes; a page is often rich with a

---

[1] *Poems*, iii., p. 10.   [2] *Ibid.*, i., p. 190.

wealth of imagery that would serve a "minor"
writer for a volume. That Holmes is a true
poet is a matter about which there cannot be
any doubt, despite the fact that many persons
would add, "Yes, a true *humorous* poet,"—implying
in their use of the word humorous a something
derogatory to the man's genius as a poet. Yes, he
is a humorous poet; and in the peculiar sense of
being a true poet and a great humourist combined
we can only find his equal in Thomas Hood.
Although both as poets and as humourists they
were quite unlike, still in the peculiar combination
of the two functions they are the same. They are
not poets, without the saving quality of humour;
they are not versifying humourists like a Coleman,
a Hook, or a W. S. Gilbert, who are humourists
merely using the poetic vehicle stripped of all that
makes it poetry. Holmes is a didactic poet, not

> "dealing counsel from a lofty height
> That makes the lowly hate it,"

but using his poetry as a means to teach men the
truths that have come to him as one of themselves,
and it is the *entente cordiale* consequently established between writer and readers that makes
him so widely loved. It is not often in his pages
that we light upon a purely imaginative poem,
such as *The Chambered Nautilus* and *Musa* and a
few more, but when we do we are sure to find that

they bear instant evidence of their origin in the alembic of a pure poet's soul. Of the combination of humour and pathos referred to we have frequent examples in that most striking series of *vers d'occasion* entitled in the collected works, *Poems of the Class of* '29. This series, which extended from 1851 until 1889, while giving us examples of many different moods, has yet running like a silver thread through all a bright, unfailing, humour-loving optimism. After reading, one year, a half-regretful musing over their long past, their " class poet " would come before " The Boys," as he called them, with a rousing verse of humour :—

" I like full well the deep resounding swell
  Of mighty symphonies with chords inwoven ;
But sometimes, too, a song of Burns—don't you ?
  After a solemn storm-blast of Beethoven.

" Good to the heels the well-worn slipper feels
  When the tired player shuffles off the buskin ;
A page of Hood may do a fellow good
  After a scolding from Carlyle or Ruskin." [1]

The very next year we have a really pathetic picture called up before us of the last survivor of the class :—

" Yes ! the vacant chairs tell sadly we are going, going fast,
And the thought comes strangely o'er me, who will live to be the last ?
    *   *   *   *   *

---

[1] *Poems*, ii., p. 73.

His figure shows but dimly, his face I scarce can see,—
There's something that reminds me,—it looks like—is it
   he?
He? Who? No voice may whisper what wrinkled brow
   shall claim
The wreath of stars that circles our last survivor's name." [1]

Celebrated as they thus have been by the greatest of their number the members of the Harvard Class of '29 will enjoy a unique fame, for the poems written for their anniversary meeting are something far better in quality than we are accustomed to associate with poetical work produced in such circumstances.

   " Year by year, like milestones placed,
    Mark the record Friendship traced.
    Prisoned in the walls of time
    Life has notched itself in rhyme." [2]

Holmes's occasional verse is really remarkable for its combination of the qualities which characterise the rest of his poetry—one becomes aware at once that the poems are no laboured task which the poet has badgered his brains to produce for the stated occasion, but are the fresh outpourings of a cheerful, healthy and remarkably ready poetic nature. Some beautiful pieces celebrate various Harvard anniversaries, other than those connected with the class of '29, meetings of alumni, etc. The "old boy" tells them, in verses always containing

---

[1] *Poems*, ii., p. 78.　　　[2] *Ibid.*, ii., p. 201.

an undercurrent of deep thought, what they dreamed of when young, and what has come in the shape of experience with the gathering years—

" We've seen the little tricks of life, its varnish and veneer,
Its stucco-fronts of character flake off and disappear,
We've learned that oft the brownest hands will heap the biggest pile,
And met with many a 'perfect brick' beneath a rimless 'tile.'

" What dreams we've had of deathless name, as scholars, statesmen, bards,
While Fame, the lady with the trump, held up her picture cards !
Till, having nearly played our game, she gaily whispered, 'Ah !
I said you should be something grand,—you'll soon be grandpapa.' " [1]

In 1836 on the celebration of the two-hundredth anniversary of Harvard, Holmes—*felix audacia*—sang a song of his own. Fifty years later, at a similar celebration, he read a long poem, full of the fire, fervour, and character which we find in his earlier work. Whenever such occasions have arisen during his long life, Holmes has been called upon to celebrate the event in verse, and not alone on such occasions, but also on innumerable minor and more private ones, at times when people were gathered together to hail the coming, speed the

[1] *Poems*, i., p. 265.

parting guest. Preluding *Songs of Many Seasons*
in 1874 the poet himself said,—

> " Not for glory, not for pelf,
> Not, be sure, to please myself,
> Not for any meaner ends,—
> Always ' by request of friends.'

> " Here's the cousin of a King,—
> Would I do the civil thing?
> Here's the first-born of a Queen :
> Here's a slant-eyed Mandarin.

> " *Would* I polish off Japan ?
> *Would* I greet this famous man,
> Prince or Prelate, Sheik or Shah ?—
> Figaro çi and Figaro là !

> " *Would* I just this once comply ?—
> So they teased and teased till I
> (Be the truth at once confessed)
> Wavered—yielded—did my best." [1]

Even in his lighter poems, those dealing with
essentially humorous subjects, or those with which
he delighted after-dinner audiences, we have
evidence that, as he expresses it, while his gay
stanzas

> "pleased the banquet's lords,
> The soul within was tuned to deeper chords ! " [2]

Among the humorous poems which we find in
Holmes's three volumes several have for many
years been favourites of readers and reciters at

---

[1] *Poems*, ii., p. 201.   [2] *Ibid.*, i., p. 109.

popular entertainments—such, for instance, as the *Deacon's Masterpiece ; or, The Wonderful " One-Hoss Shay,"* [1] a poem which may well stand as representative of the best expression of American humour. This is, however, but one of many poems which might be included in the same category. In these poems humour has been the *motif*, while in many others humour is used as a light the better to throw up the meaning which the author wishes to convey—as the jam of sweetness in which the doctor-poet often disguises a powder of teaching. Humour is certainly one of the essential factors in the constitution of Holmes's genius, although he can at times wax deadly serious when combating what appears to him as humbug or meanness, writing even with scathing satire at times, as when he addressed a poem, during the inter-States struggle, to *The Sweet Little Man*, and dedicated it to the " Stay-at-Home Rangers "—

" Bring him the buttonless garment of woman !
   Cover his face lest it freckle and tan ;
Muster the Apron-String Guards on the Common,
   That is the corps for the sweet little man !" [2]

This satiric turn to his humour is frequently given in snatches of his song, as though the philosopher were driving a truth home with a weapon lent him by the poet. Of the pen he says in *The*

---

[1] *Poems*, ii., p. 131.   [2] *Ibid.*, ii., p. 236.

Schoolboy, a song which celebrated the centennial
of Phillips's Academy,—[1]

> " Too ready servant, whose deceitful ways
> Full many a slip-shod line, alas ! betrays ;
> Hence of the rhyming thousand not a few
> Have builded worse—a great deal—than they knew." [2]

Or we may take a passage such as this from a
poem read at a Medical Society dinner—

> " Strong is the moral blister that will draw
> Laid on the conscience of the Man of Law,
> Whom blindfold Justice lends her eyes to see
> Truth in the scale that holds his promised fee." [3]

Or this, from verses addressed to James Russell
Lowell, where we have a very happy use made of
one of the most famous lines from *Chevy Chase*—

> " And if we lose him our lament will be
> We have ' five hundred '—*not* ' as good as he.' " [3]

Of humour pure and simple, the humour of
extravagance or of fun, we have many examples
scattered up and down the pages.

> " A health to stout Hans Breitmann ! How long before
> we see
> Another Hans as handsome,—as bright a man as he ! " [5]

Of the grand new gilded dome of Boston, " the hub
of the solar system," he says—

---

[1] See *ante*, p. 6.   [3] *Poems*, iii., p. 112.
[2] *Poems*, iii., p. 94.   [4] *Ibid.*, iii., p. 135.
[5] *Ibid.*, iii., 157.

" When first in his path a young asteroid found it,
　As he sailed through the skies with the stars in his
　　wake,
He thought 'twas the sun, and kept circling around it
　Till Edison signalled, ' You've made a mistake.' " [1]

In reading many of these purely humorous
ebullitions of playful fancy, it seems difficult to
realise that they are by the poet who could at
times touch the lyre with such very different effect.
It is interesting to notice that during the first
years of his poethood Holmes wrote some of the
most wildly humorous and at the same time some
of the most obviously serious of his work. The
transition from the one to the other is probably
but natural—youth knows no " happy mean," if
the term be not inaccurate—it is wildly playful,
or, when serious, it is so in deadly earnest. In
middle and later life the poet has apparently
realised that his work has received most attention,
and therefore, it is to be presumed, has had most
effect, when he has succeeded in subtly fusing the
two qualities in such a way as he has made
familiar to us in a great number of his poems.
It has been said that we have to go back to the
date of Dryden and Pope, or at least to that of
Goldsmith, for poetry to which that of Holmes
is most akin. In his didactic couplets we may
perhaps frequently find passages suggestive of the

---

[1] *Poems*, iii., p. 81.

earlier writers, and for forceful directness, combined with simplicity of expression, we might find
many lines parallel with those of Oliver Goldsmith. The humour of Dryden and Pope was
the grim humour of the satirist, and not of that
harmless kind whose lambent light plays around
so much of Holmes's writings. With Goldsmith,
the kinship is perhaps somewhat closer, although
the resources of the more modern poet-doctor—
for did not Goldy, too, write himself M.D.?—are
more plentiful, and his wide and various knowledge
of men gives him an advantage over poor Nolly.

Holmes's faculty for seizing upon similes and
allusions is extraordinary and perhaps unequalled.
Thomas Moore plumed himself on a friend having
totted up the similes in his *Life of Sheridan*, the
abundance of which, said the self-satisfied singer,
was strong evidence of his poetic nature; as
though it was necessary that the writer of *Lalla
Rookh* and the *Irish Melodies* should have compiled
a *Life of Sheridan* to prove that he was a poet!
The friend who should set about so thankless a
task for Oliver Wendell Holmes would at any rate
be able to produce a very large total on the com-
pletion of his misapplied labours. In this regard,
Lowell, perhaps, may run Holmes rather close, for
he also possesses in a remarkable degree the power
of instantly calling up illustrations to point that
which he may be saying; for instance, how very

beautiful yet how unexpected is the simile in this verse describing Huldy in the later versions of *The Courtin'* !—

> " For she was jest the quiet kind
> Whose naturs never vary,
> Like streams that keep a summer mind
> Snow-hid in Jenooary."

How happy, too, is the same writer's allusion in the *Biglow Papers* !—

> " We begin to think it's nater
> To take sarse an' not be riled ;—
> Who'd expect to see a tater
> All on eend at bein' biled ? " [1]

Every page that Holmes has written, of prose or poetry, reveals his possession of this power in a remarkable degree—a power which must have gone far to give his work the high place which it holds in the regard of present readers, and to which it will probably owe much of its fame in years to come. We may glance at one or two illustrative examples of what is here insisted upon. In describing the difference between the time of youth and of age he tells us that—

> " The hearts that were thumping like ships on the rocks
> Beat as quiet and steady as meeting-house clocks." [2]

[1] J. R. Lowell: *Collected Works*, vol. viii., p. 45.
[2] *Poems*, ii., p. 66.

" Stick to your aim : the mongrel's hold will slip,
But only crowbars loose the bulldog's grip." [1]

" On the blue flower a bluer flower you spy,
You stretch to pluck it—'tis a butterfly ;
The flattened tree-toads so resemble bark,
They're hard to find as Ethiops in the dark;
The woodcock, stiffening to fictitious mud,
Cheats the young sportsman thirsting for his blood ;
So by long living on a single lie,
Nay, on one truth, will creatures get its dye." [2]

" Women, with tongues
Like polar needles, ever on the jar ;
Men, plugless word-spouts, whose deep fountains are
Within their lungs." [3]

" Time is the angel-thief which Nature sends us
To break the cramping fetters of our past." [4]

" How the past spreads out in vision with its far-receding
train,
Like a long-embroidered arras in the chambers of the
brain." [5]

It will be seen at once by these few examples how
readily the poet lays hold of similes quite apposite,
yet, entirely unhackneyed and unspoiled by endless
repetition, they come upon us as we read with all
the pleasure of that surprise which is said to lie at
the root of our delight in wit.

It is very obvious that Holmes's work contrasts

[1] *Poems*, i., p. 121.   [3] *Poems*, i., p. 16.
[2] *Ibid.*, i., p. 207.   [4] *Ibid.*, ii., p. 103.
[5] *Ibid.*, ii., p. 81.

very sharply with that of those morbidly melancholy "albino-poets," as he terms them, "whose
refrain is 'I shall die and be forgotten, and the
world will go on just as if I had never been;—
yet how I have loved! how I have longed! how
I have aspired!'"[1]

There is, perhaps, no commoner—and at the
same time there is no more dangerous form of
criticism than that which attempts to forecast the
view which the Future (capitalised) will take of
a given piece of work, or the works of a given
author. The criticism which consists in saying,
"This will live when Homer is forgotten"—"and
not *till* then," as a wit is reported to have added—
is of course sweeping, but it is—if one may be
permitted the apparent Hibernianism—sweepingly
inconclusive; it is given with an air of assurance
which is begotten of the fact that the critic knows
that until the Future has become the Present—in
other words until "Homer is forgotten"—his judgment though it may be called in question cannot
be refuted. It is true that the work so welcomed
may be forgotten during the lifetime of both critic
and author,—"'tis nothing," says the critic—the
author, of course, saying "Ditto, to Mr. Burke"—
while triumphantly pointing to great works which
Fame, the jilt, has studiously neglected for long

[1] *Autocrat*, p. 185.

periods and then welcomed with a smile of recognition and taken into her favour. The work hailed with delight and ranked with the greatest is perchance soon forgotten, it becomes that nine-days' wonder, that thing for which the writer for cash must pray day and night, and for which the true literary artist must as earnestly pray may not be his—"the book of the season." Such as a topical song is to music, as a daily illustrated paper is to art, so is, most often, the book of the season to literature—it is for a season and *not* for all time. Another book, published it may be at the very same time, has fallen foul of the critics, or has fallen, apparently, stillborn from the press, and is yet destined to be one of the books of the world.

I will not say of Holmes that he will be remembered when Homer is forgotten ; we may, however, consider the position which he occupies among his contemporaries—the leading men of letters of America. "Who"—asked Sydney Smith, in a famous review—"Who in all the four Continents reads an American book?" The century has seen great changes, and to-day we ask, "What English publisher does not profit by pirating American books for British readers?" Holmes's works alone are procurable from half a dozen publishers other than the firm which issues his authorised collected edition. As a poet, the position which rightfully belongs to Holmes is immediately after Long-

fellow in point of fame, while in point of popularity he is probably to-day the very first. It
may yet be true, as has been suggested, that his
work is less likely to live—through being scattered over so many short pieces—through there
being no one great poem to remember him by—and
through so much of it being written for certain
stated occasions.

III.

THE NOVELIST.

FILLING AN ORDER.

(Read at the Holmes' Breakfast, December 3rd, 1879.)

BY J. T. TROWBRIDGE.

To Nature, in her shop one day, at work compounding
simples,
Studying fresh tints for Beauty's cheeks, or new effects in
dimples,
An order came : she wiped in haste her fingers and un-
folded
The scribbled scrap, put on her specs, and read it while
she scolded.

" From Miss Columbia ! I declare ! of all the upstart
misses !
What will the jade be asking next ? Now what an order
this is !
Where's Boston ? Oh, that one-horse town out there beside
the ocean !
She wants—of course, she always wants—another little
notion !

" This time, three geniuses, A1 ! to grace her favourite
city :
The first, a bard ; the second, wise ; the third, supremely
witty ;

None of the staid and hackneyed sort, but some peculiar
    flavour,
Something unique and fresh for each will be esteemed a
    favour !
Modest demands ! as if my hands had but to turn and
    toss over
A Poet veined with dew and fire, a Wit, and a Philo-
    sopher !

"But now, let's see !" She put aside her old, outworn
    expedients,
And in a quite unusual way began to mix ingredients,—
Some in the fierce retort distilled, some pounded by the
    pestle,—
And set the simmering souls to steep, each in its glowing
    vessel.
In each, by turns, she poured, she stirred, she skimmed
    the shining liquor,
Threw laughter in to make it thin, or thought, to make it
    thicker.
But when she came to choose the clay, she found, to her
    vexation,
That, with a stock on hand to fill an order for a nation,
Of that more finely tempered stuff, electric and ethereal,
Of which a genius must be formed, she had but scant
    material—
For three? For one ! What should be done? A bright
    idea struck her ;
Her old witch-eyes began to shine, her mouth began to
    pucker.
Says she, "The fault, I'm well aware, with genius is the
    presence
Of altogether too much clay, with quite too little
    essence,
And sluggish atoms that obstruct the spiritual solution ;
So now, instead of spoiling these by over much dilution,

With their fine elements I'll make a single, rare pheno-
  menon,
And of three common geniuses concoct a most uncommon
  one,
So that the world shall smile to see a soul so universal,
Such poesy and pleasantry, packed in so small a parcel."

So said, so done ; the three in one she wrapped, and
  stuck the label :
Poet, Professor, Autocrat of Wit's own Breakfast-Table.

IN glancing over the facts of Holmes's life it was
  seen that he did not become a novelist until he
had reached the mature age of half a century—an
almost unprecedented instance of deferred develop-
ment of a talent.   It is, of course, true that during
the two years which preceded the first appearance
of *Elsie Venner*, the author had been writing a
kind of fiction in the first two-thirds of the *Breakfast-Table Series.*   He had, however, made no
effort at a sustained plot and the consecutive
arraying of events round certain individuals
which we have come to look upon as essential in
the novel ; therefore, despite the Professor's and
Schoolmistress's romance we can scarcely classify
the earlier works with the three volumes of fiction,
although we find in the former many of the dis-
tinguishing qualities of the latter.   It is, however,
just those qualities of the *causeur* which charm
us in the Breakfast-Table speaker that, on the
whole, detract from the value of the novel, both as

an example of the art of fiction, and as a mere story. The most obvious of these qualities is discursiveness —the discursiveness of desultory conversation which from one subject passes on to another with such fine connecting threads, that those who are speaking are often ignorant of the conversational short-cuts which have taken them, perchance within three minutes, from discussing the dresses worn at the Drawing Room to the prospects of the whale fishery. This method of telling a story—a perennial source of delight in the gossiping philosophy of the Autocrat and the Professor—borders upon the irritating when we are reading *Elsie Venner*, *The Guardian Angel*, and, most of all, *A Mortal Antipathy*.

A series of articles appeared in a London magazine several years ago in which the writer—appropriately named N. E. Howe—started off with the intention of getting to Tottenham Court Road ; one subject led to another, until he found himself very far afield at the conclusion of each article, and in each succeeding paper made a fresh start, with, of course, a similar result. This went on for many weeks, but whether Mr. N. E. Howe succeeded eventually in reaching Tottenham Court Road my memory refuses to divulge. I am often reminded in reading Holmes of those *Higgledy-Piggledy Papers*, for at times the story gets almost lost sight of while the *raconteur*

indulges himself in a bit of more or less relevant
scientific disquisition, personal reminiscence, or
curious book-lore; the chapter is then brought to
an end and the thread of the story retaken up at
the commencement of the next.   Although this is,
artistically, a fault, it is one which the charm of
Holmes's style helps to minimise, and which to a
certain extent his readers anticipate from him as
the dilettante speaker of the breakfast-table.   Woe
unto the young fictionist who should essay the
same discursiveness !

Holmes's novels form three of the thirteen volumes
of his collected works; they are, *Elsie Venner :
a Romance of Destiny* (originally called *The Professor's Story*), 1860 ; *The Guardian Angel* (in a
subtle sense a sequel to the earlier work), 1867 ;
and, nearly twenty years later, *A Mortal Antipathy*
in 1885.   Each of these three books is remarkable,
and each more or less in the same ways—remarkable, that is, in the bold originality of plot for
stories dealing with modern life, in the delicate
and skilful handling of delicate subjects, in the
strong portrayal of individual characters, and in
the thought-laden sentences which build up the
story and which *may* often be read by the seeker
for a mere story oblivious of the fact that they are
any more significant than the sentences which build
up the average three-volume novel—such readers,
that is, as would, to use Doctor Holmes's own illus-

tration, read *Æsop's Fables* and skip the morals. The novels are obviously the work of a doctor and of a poet—though the young aspirant to the poet's bays gets somewhat severely treated in the character of Gifted Hopkins in *The Guardian Angel*. The professional man has not only supplied the leading idea for each story, but here and there the reader observes in every chapter the technical knowledge cropping out. The ready profusion of imagery and similes, a characteristic which we have treated earlier, is essentially that of a poetic nature.

In saying that the doctor has supplied the leading idea for each of these three stories, we have already indicated that they are "novels with a purpose." Now this class of fiction has to-day become so common, and, perhaps, so abused, an institution, that if on picking up a new work we find it stated early in the preface that "through all the disguise of fiction a grave scientific (social, moral or theological, according to the bent of the writer) doctrine may be detected," most of us, it is to be suspected, would drop the book in disgust, and take up by preference a story that aimed at being nothing more. The "novel with a purpose" during the first half of the present century had been mainly concerned with showing how, despite all trials, goodness and virtue were sure to triumph over badness and vice; that

although the course of true love never did run
smooth during the first four hundred and ninety-
nine pages, so soon as the hero and heroine had
reached the five-hundredth page they got on to a
perfectly level track, and all went smoothly afterwards; the path to the church door was shown
full of deadly dangers, the road was of the
roughest, storms lowered, villains and false lovers
were at every turn ready to effect some (always
foiled) deadly purpose to thwart the onward journey
of the devoted lovers; stern, unsympathising
parents and guardians with their attendant tools
grew "thick as weeds" on the way; but—the
church door once attained, the hero and heroine
when they came out again found all was changed;
the sun shone brilliantly, the birds sang, the easy
pleasant path "wound on through vistas of the
future" (whatever that might mean), while every
person that was met proved a friend and a bene-
factor, and—and "they all lived happily ever
after." Such was the novel that gladdened the
hearts and improved the morals of our great-
grandparents; but, *nous avons changé tout cela*;
now the novel with a purpose gives us an unimpeded
short-cut through the first three chapters to the
church (or registry office), the hero and heroine are
married, or perhaps one of them to the wrong person,
and then begins the course that is not smooth.

This is, perhaps, taking somewhat extreme

instances, for it is an undoubted fact that many novels with a purpose have effectively fulfilled that purpose. Novels of this order are, however, of widely differing varieties. From the social reform novels of some years ago—inaugurated, or at any rate considerably strengthened, by Charles Dickens—we have at length got to the fashionable religious-problem, or marriage-problem novel of recent date. It is an interesting question—although one which the critic of the future will alone be competent to answer satisfactorily—as to how far a novelist curtails his fame, in point of time, by dealing with problems of the moment. It seems reasonable to suppose that the generations of readers who come after the solution of the problem will take but a slight, and ever lessening, interest in works the reason for whose being is the statement of a position which they probably are unable to realise. To put the question shortly, and by example,—will not the novels told for the sake of the romance, say those of Walter Scott, outlast in popularity the novels with a purpose, to give another foremost example, of Charles Dickens?

Doctor Holmes's are essentially novels with a purpose; though the problems with which they deal are of much more than mere temporary interest; yet the fact that they are such, is likely to militate against them as living works of art.

The problem which is dealt with in the first of the three novels—*Elsie Venner*—is as to how far an individual, suffering from hereditary or other pre-natal bias, is a responsible being and answerable to ordinary moral or human law as a free agent. In a note in a late edition of the *Professor at the Breakfast-Table*, the author evidenced his lasting interest in such a problem. A discussion had arisen at the breakfast-table over a line in one of Holmes's own poems,—

" Don't be ' consistent '—but be simply *true*." [1]

" The more I have observed and reflected," he went on to say, "the more limited seems to me the field of action of the human will. Every act of choice involves a special relation between the *ego* and the conditions before it. But no man knows what forces are at work in the determination of his *ego*. The bias which decides his choice between two or more motives, may come from some unsuspected ancestral source, of which he knows nothing at all. He is automatic in virtue of that hidden spring of reflex action, all the time having the feeling that he is self-determining. The story of *Elsie Venner*, written soon after this book was published, illustrates the direction in which my thought was moving. The imaginary subject of the story obeyed her *will*, but her will

---

[1] *Poems*, i., p. 121.

obeyed the mysterious ante-natal poisoning influence." This passage is also worth remembering in reading *The Guardian Angel*. The story of *Elsie Venner* ran in serial form through the pages of the *Atlantic Monthly* as *The Professor's Love Story*, and only received its present name on republication as a volume. The story seems in its main theme to be wildly improbable, if not impossible; it, however, enabled the author, as he expressed it later, "to suggest the limitations of human responsibility in a simple and effective way"; [1] it reads like some old legend—such as that dealt with by Keats in *Lamia*, or, more recently, by Dr. Garnett in *The Poison Maid*—in fact, some readers have imagined it to be a modern romance structure erected on an ancient foundation. However, the author himself says, "My poor heroine found her origin, not in fable or romance, but in a physiological conception fertilised by a theological dogma." [2]

The idea of an animal nature subtly blent with the human is a very old one. Holmes, in his second preface to this book, refers to Hawthorne's *Marble Faun*, written about the same time and published while *Elsie Venner* was appearing in the *Atlantic Monthly*, and also to Keats's *Lamia*. Keats's story is taken from a passage in Burton's

---

[1] *The Guardian Angel*, p. vii. [2] *Elsie Venner*, p. x.

Anatomy of Melancholy, which again is taken from Philostratus' fourth book, *De Vita Apollonii*, so that the idea is a sufficiently old one. Holmes, however, as will be shown, writes on this subject not so much with the object of telling an intensely tragical story, as of putting a definite problem.

When this work was published Doctor Holmes had turned his half-century, and although it may appear remarkable that a man should commence being novelist at so mature an age, it must be borne in mind that the book, although a novel—a romance of destiny as it is called—is yet something more and at the same time something less than a novel as that term is generally accepted. The author had shown himself in the *Autocrat* and the *Professor* as a delightful *raconteur*, and really in the novel we can see the Professor behind it all. The strangely mysterious destiny of Elsie herself is terribly tragic; the steady diamond glitter of her eyes is present to the reader all through the work. Where the author can give his pathetic humour play we get some beautiful pieces of character drawing; even though the persons portrayed are but minor individuals in the action, yet they live for us more really than do some of the more fully developed ones; the unrelievedly pathetic side of life is not quite so successfully dealt with, except perhaps in the case of poor, long-suffering Helen Darley, who is made to live for us, and to claim our sympathy, as only genius can make its puppets. As with the characters, so with the book as a piece of literary workmanship, —looking at the words in which the story is told— it is most excellent where humour and pathos are delicately intermingled one with the other. Another striking feature, here as elsewhere, is Holmes's extraordinary wealth of similes, and the depth of thought which he shows throughout in dealing with such difficult subjects as heredity, sin, and other phases of moral responsibility.

"It is very singular that we recognise all the bodily defects that unfit a man for military service, and all the intellectual ones that limit his range of thought, but always talk at him as if all his moral powers were perfect. I suppose we must punish evil-doers as we extirpate vermin; but I don't know that we have any more right to judge them than we have to judge rats and mice, which are just as good as cats and weasels, though we think it necessary to treat them as criminals." [1] This passage, both in thought and feeling, is expressive of much which we shall find in the novels of Oliver Wendell Holmes.

Elsie Venner opens, characteristically enough, with a dissertation on the state of caste which has gradually grown up in democratic America—by

---

[1] *Elsie Venner*, p. 226.

which an observer may know at once whether a
given man belongs to the classes whose members
have been educated for centuries, or whether he is
one of the many who have not had generations of
University training—it is, indeed, an insistence
upon the fact of there being in the States both
classes and masses. This is merely preliminary
to the introduction of Bernard Langdon, a young
medical student who is just giving up his studies,
owing to family misfortunes, and is about to go
forth into the world. The Professor, who tells the
story, gives his whilom pupil a certificate stating
that he is a fit and proper individual to teach
persons of either sex, and from these two words
"either sex" the writer spins a whole chapter.
This is probably but the result of the habit which
he must have acquired during the previous years
of writing (*Breakfast-Table Series*) on subjects in
a conversational manner. Langdon, then, goes off
to a boys' school where the scholars are in a state
of rebellion owing to the moral and physical
weakness of previous masters—Langdon, as befits
the hero of a novel, is as strong physically and
athletically as he is morally and intellectually ; the
result is that he very soon restores order in the
rebellious school. Before his month of trial is over
he gets a better offer, and goes to the Apollinean
Institute at Rocklands, where the greater part
of the story centres. The assistant teacher of

English at the Institute is Miss Helen Darley, and among the pupils is the strangely afflicted girl, or young woman, who gives her name to the story.

Elsie is the only child of Dudley Venner, of the Dudley Mansion, a retired, taciturn man, whose wife had died in giving birth to their daughter. A short while before that happened, the young wife had been bitten fatally by a *crotalus* or rattlesnake, and the child was partially endowed with a serpent nature from the moment of her birth. The peculiar influence which, owing to her thus ophidianised character, Elsie is capable of exercising over those persons with whom she is brought into contact is more particularly observable in regard to the patient, overworked and sensitive schoolmistress—Helen Darley. No one can help noticing that there is a peculiar repellent fascination in the girl—though only her father and old Sophy the black nurse are aware of the reason for it. The general opinion is that she is, to a certain extent, mad, and so she is in being an extraordinary individuality unable to control her actions by any ordinary distinctions as to right and wrong. None, however, even suspect the terrible nature of the tragedy which is the cause of the semi-solitary life led by the occupants of the Dudley Mansion. Elsie goes and comes and does as she pleases ; visits with impunity the crotalus-haunted heights of "the mountain," even on one occasion stayed there the whole night, causing much anxiety and alarm to her father and old Sophy the nurse.

It is, of course, inevitable that the fascinating and afflicted Elsie shall develop a passion for the young master, Bernard Langdon; it is also as inevitable that the passion shall *not* be reciprocated, and that Elsie shall die. The romance is, indeed, a tragedy of which the fifth act is foreshadowed by the first. What more especially perhaps concerns us here in treating of Holmes's contributions to fictional literature is not so much the story as the working out of the root-problem from which the story grew. The author of *Elsie Venner*, in penning a second preface, says that a dear old lady friend of his declared that she would never read the book because it was " a medicated novel "; he then goes on to say, " I was always pleased with her discriminating criticism. It *is* a medicated novel, and if she wished to read for mere amusement and helpful recreation there was no need of troubling herself with a story written with a different end in view."

" The real aim of the story " (to use the author's own exposition) "was to test the doctrine of ' original sin ' and human responsibility for the disordered volition coming under that technical denomination. Was Elsie Venner, poisoned by the venom of a crotalus before she was born, morally responsible or the ' volitional ' aberrations, which, translated into acts, become what is known as sin, and, it may be, what is punished as crime? If, on presentation of the evidence, she becomes by the verdict of the human conscience a proper object of divine pity and not of divine wrath, as a subject of moral poisoning, wherein lies the difference between her position at the bar of judgment, human or divine, and that of the unfortunate victim who received a moral poison from a remote ancestor before he drew his first breath?"

It is, of course, both psychologically and morally, a most important problem which the doctor-novelist has set, and which he has answered, in this volume. Can this woman poisoned before birth be held, either by God or man, entirely responsible for her actions? Surely not. That which is sin when conceived or performed by other persons is nothing but the outcome of her natural endowments—natural, that is, in the sense of being entirely from under her own individual control. She has no perception of moral right or wrong. If crossed in anything she gives way to paroxysms of rage, and attempts to bite or deliberately to poison whosoever shall have offended. It is, taking such a case as is here indicated, impossible to make Elsie morally guilty of the crimes she may commit or attempt to commit. Having granted this it is of course inevitable that we should go one step farther, as Doctor Holmes

points out, a step which, though it may still be
startling to some readers, is this—if Elsie Venner
is to be pitied, not condemned, for her actions,
then the doctrine of individual answerability for
" original sin " is no longer tenable; and, more
than that, in any given case of crime and wrong-
doing we must be careful to make all due allowances
for transmitted tendencies in the criminal. We
must, indeed, carry the theory—if we are yet to
call it but a theory—of heredity to its only
logical conclusion; and, unless we are to punish
the hunchback for his hunch, the child born blind
for his want of sight, or the one born lame for his
lameness, we shall have to find some other method
than that of punishment for moral as well as
physical deformities. We shall have to deal with
most classes of wrong-doers as persons who are
not morally whole. This may to readers of to-
day sound somewhat trite teaching, but it must
be borne in mind that this novel was published a generation ago—and that the awaken-
ing of the public interest in such questions
during the last quarter of a century has been
very sudden. Those who have grown up during
the change are probably but slightly aware of
how great it has been.

This is dealing with the germinal idea of the
book, but apart from this, as a novel to be " read
for mere amusement and helpful recreation " it

calls for a few words. Those persons like Doctor Holmes's lady-friend whose dislike of "medicated novels" is so strong as to make them refuse to read it, will lose a great deal of enjoyment both of literary style and of sharply drawn characterisation. Some of the chapters in the book, despite the intensely tragic motive of the work, are pure comedy—those, for example, that deal with Colonel Sprowle and his family—all of whom are apparently introduced merely for the purpose of giving the author an opportunity of heightening the effect of the money-making meanness of Silas Peckham, the ignorant, vulgar, and calculating manager of the Rocklands Apollinean "Institoot." The Sprowles had given a great and ostentatious party to which "everybody was invited," when on the following morning Silas Peckham goes round to "the Colonel's"—

"'Colonel Sprowle,' said he, 'there's meat and cakes and pies and pickles enough on that table to spread a hahnsome cōlation. If you'd like to trade reasonable, I think perhaps I should be willin' to take 'em off your hands. There's been a talk about our havin' a celebration in the Parnassian Grove, and I think I could work in what your folks don't want and make myself whole by chargin' a small sum for tickets. Broken meats, of course, a'n't of the same valoo as fresh provisions; so I think you might be willin' to trade reasonable.'

"Mr. Peckham paused and rested on his pro-
posal. It would not, perhaps, have been very
extraordinary, if Colonel Sprowle had entertained
the proposition. There is no telling beforehand
how such things will strike people. It didn't
happen to strike the Colonel favourably. He had
a little red-blooded manhood in him.

"'Sell you them things to make a cōlation out
of?' the Colonel replied. 'Walk up to that table,
Mr. Peckham, and help yourself! Fill your pockets,
Mr. Peckham! Fetch a basket, and our hired
folks shall fill it full for ye! Send a cart, if
y' like, 'n' carry off them leavin's to make a celebration for your pupils with! Only let me tell
ye this:—as sure's my name's Hezekiah Spraowle,
you'll be known through the taown, 'n' through
the caounty, from that day forrard, as the Principal
of the Broken-Victuals Institoot!'

"Even provincial human nature sometimes has
a touch of sublimity about it. Mr. Silas Peckham
had gone a little deeper than he meant, and come
upon the 'hard pan,' as the well-diggers call it,
of the Colonel's character, before he thought of it.
A militia colonel standing on his sentiments is not
to be despised. . . .

"Mr. Silas Peckham said little or nothing. His
sensibilities were not acute, but he perceived that
he had made a miscalculation. He hoped that
there was no offence,—thought it might have been

mutooally agreeable, conclooded he would give up the idee of a cōlation, and backed himself out as if unwilling to expose the less guarded aspect of his person to the risk of accelerating impulses.

"The Colonel shut the door,—cast his eye on the toe of his right boot, as if it had had a strong temptation,—looked at his watch, then round the room, and, going to a cupboard, swallowed a glass of deep-red brandy and water to compose his feelings."[1]

The whole of the long chapter which describes the Sprowles' party is deliciously humorous, though its connection with the story is but very slight. Contrasting passages of pathos are more numerous in the romance than these comedy scenes; this however is not suprising, for out of the four heroes and heroines in whom our interest chiefly centres, one alone—Bernard Langdon—can be called a normally healthy individual; Elsie, we have seen, was sorely afflicted; her father was forced, by grief for his young dead wife and living daughter, to the life of a solitary and recluse; Helen Darley led an overworked and unloved life of loneliness. Besides these leading characters, however, *Elsie Venner* presents us with quite a number of persons of minor import who are yet sharply and completely characterised by their author—they stand clearly in our memory as

---

[1] *Elsie Venner*, pp. 131-3.

though we had met and conversed with them in
the flesh. Such characters, for example, as the
Yankee school principal, Silas Peckham, ever
thinking of profit-making; Colonel Sprowle and his
family, again, with their moneyed vulgarity, are
portrayed with the satiric realism of a Thackeray;
then there are the two antipodean reverends—Dr.
Honeywood and Chauncey Fairweather,—each of
whose characters and teaching is slightly indicated
in his name, the former being the kindly, brotherly
pastor—man first, and then clergyman, while the
other is a strict dogmatist, shivering ever on the
brink of Romanism; Abel Stebbins the Doctor's
Man, Widow Marilla Rowens, Elsie's Cousin
Richard, Old Sophy the black nurse, are all
clearly individualised and well-rounded character-
conceptions which serve to impart much interest
and amusing by-play to the more sombre central
features of the volume.

In *The Guardian Angel* we are again brought
face to face with a novel, the story of which is the
working out of a curious problem in psychology.
In the preface the author refers to the various
readers of fables—the many that read for the sake
of the story to the one who reads for the sake of
the moral. It is as easy, he suggests, to read his
novels and ignore the problems, as it is to read
Æsop's Fables and skip the morals. With some
readers—they must be accomplished " skippers,"—

this may be, but Doctor Holmes has paid no very great compliment to their perspicacity in saying so, especially when we consider the various references which are made to the problem lying at the root of the story. For example, of the infant Myrtle Hazard, we are told that "the instincts and qualities belonging to the ancestral traits which predominated in the conflict of mingled lives lay in this child in embryo, waiting to come to maturity. It was as when several grafts, bearing fruit that ripens at different times, are growing upon the same stock. Her earlier impulses may have been derived directly from her father and mother, but all the ancestors who have been mentioned, and more or less obscurely many others, came uppermost in their time, before the absolute and total result of their several forces had found its equilibrium in the character by which she was to be known as an individual. These inherited impulses were therefore many, conflicting, some of them dangerous. The World, the Flesh, and the Devil held mortgages on her life before its deed was put in her hands; but sweet and gracious influences were also born with her; and the battle of life was to be fought between them, God helping her in her need, and her own free choice siding with one or the other." [1] Every reader—even one who

_____

[1] *The Guardian Angel*, pp. 26-7.

leaves the reading of the preface until he has finished the story—has very frequently brought to his consciousness the nature of the problem which is stated.

Writing in 1891 the author says, "The principle of heredity has been largely studied since this story was written. This tale, like *Elsie Venner*, depends for its deeper significance on the ante-natal history of its subject. But the story was meant to be readable for those who did not care for its underlying philosophy."[1] Probably Doctor Holmes is right: to that section of readers who do not seek for deeper thought, who take short swallow-flights of reading, and dip their wings in fiction and fly away, the story, apart from its philosophy, has doubtless proved, and will yet prove, attractive; some, like the lady who declined to read *Elsie Venner*, will probably refuse to read this also, because it seeks to be something more than a novel.

This story—as a story—has not the tragic interest of the earlier one. The terrible "destiny" overshadowing Elsie Venner does not influence the life of the heroine of this book; the germ theme of the earlier work, was a consideration of how far the individual was himself responsible for thoughts and actions, the direct outcome of an extraordinary pre-natal influence. In *The Guardian Angel*, on the

---

[1] *The Guardian Angel,* p. xiv.

other hand, though the question of responsibility is yet the root one—it is pictured in the actions of a girl who shows in a remarkable degree the various qualities and characteristics of a mixed ancestry. It is a more familiar case of hereditary predisposition—or a more familiar exposition of the science of heredity. The chief idea out of which *The Guardian Angel* arose is given thus, early in the story :—" It is by no means certain that our individual personality is the single inhabitant of these our corporeal frames. Nay, there is recorded an experience of one of the living persons mentioned in this narrative which, so far as it is received in evidence, tends to show that some, at least, who have long been dead, may enjoy a kind of secondary and imperfect, yet self-conscious life, in these bodily tenements which we are in the habit of considering exclusively our own. There are many circumstances, familiar to common observers, which favour this belief to a certain extent. Thus, at one moment we detect the look, at another the tone of voice, at another some characteristic movement of this or that ancestor, in our relations or others. There are times when our friends do not act like themselves, but apparently in obedience to some other law than that of their own proper nature. We all do things both awake and asleep which surprise us. Perhaps we have co-tenants in this house we live in. No

less than eight distinct personalities are said to
have co-existed in a single female mentioned by an
ancient physician of unimpeachable authority.   In
this light we may perhaps see the meaning of a
sentence, from a work which will be repeatedly
referred to in this narrative—viz.: ' *This body
in which we journey across the isthmus between
the two oceans is not a private carriage, but an
omnibus.*' " [1]

The " Guardian Angel" is " Ann Holyoake,
burned by ye bloudy Papists, año 15—," as she is
described on an old picture.   Her spirit is said to
exercise over her descendants a kindly watchful-
ness; and Myrtle Hazard, the heroine of the story,
places an especial faith in this family superstition
owing to a resemblance between the portrait and a
miniature which she possesses of her dead mother.
Several of her ancestors are described, and one
grandmother was " said to have a few drops of
aboriginal blood in her veins."   She is born in
India and sent back, an orphan infant, to New
England to the care of an aunt entirely unfitted
for the charge.

It is the story of the life and love of this girl

---

[1] *The Guardian Angel*, pp. 22-3.   The supposititious
work from which this sentence is taken is by Byles
Gridley, A.M.   This kind of literary fiction had already
been most successfully inaugurated and employed by Mr.
George Meredith in *The Egoist, Richard Feverel*, etc.

which is told in this volume—a story less tense
in its tragic interest, but certainly more pleasant,
and from a "medicated" point of view more
satisfactory than its predecessor. Every person
with whom we are brought into contact—we ourselves—are each representative, so to speak, of any
number of ancestors. "Live folks are only dead
folks warmed over," as old Doctor Hurlbut is made
to say;[1] and every one of us probably shows this
more or less definitely, more especially perhaps
during the earlier part of our lives, before the sum of
inherited characteristics has been correctly totalled
up into a distinct individuality.

The various sides of Myrtle's character—the
contribution of this or that forebear—are of course
so brought out as to serve the purpose of the story.
But with the story as such—it treats of the
courses of true love which, naturally, did not run
smooth—I am not here concerned; to detail the
plot and, in short, to summarise the story comes
not within the scope of my criticism. Those who
have read the book will know it, those who have
not will scarcely like to have the edge taken off
their interest in the work as a piece of fiction.

The motive of *The Guardian Angel* is less frequently insisted upon than is that of *Elsie Venner*,
and this it is which tends to make the later the

---

[1] *The Guardian Angel*, p. 129.

more effective piece of artistic work. We are not so
often pulled up to consider the different hereditary
influences acting upon the lovable Myrtle Hazard
at various crises in her career as we are by references to the ophidianised nature of poor afflicted
Elsie Venner. Yet the varying character of the
girl is so subtly portrayed that we do not consider
the changes as inconsistencies so much as develop-
ments. Even when in the school tableaux she
is almost betrayed by passion—she is posing as
Pocahontas—into murdering one of her schoolmates,
we do not feel so shocked as we should have done
if the author's treatment of his subject had not
prepared us for such a proof of the survival in her
of something of an aboriginal ancestor. We get
so far carried away as to go the whole length of
denying the individual responsibility, and this of
course is precisely what the theorist of heredity
in the guise of a tale-teller has wished us to do.

As a story the second is more interesting than
the first, it is more artistically complete in its
working ; less broken up by only slightly pertinent
matter ; it has more humanity in it, and, though
less tragic, appeals more successfully to our sympathies and interests.

In *A Mortal Antipathy*, daringly called by its
seventy-five-year-old author " *First* Opening of the
New Portfolio," we have, as he calls it, a truly
hazardous experiment. Again, a strange psycho-

logical and pathological problem serves as the main-spring for the volume ; a problem which has long exercised the minds of men. As old probably as any of the stories of foreign natures mixed with the human is that of " antipathies," the instinctive and unreasonable dislike of some persons to some other persons or things—

> " Some men there are love not a gaping pig;
> Some that are mad if they behold a cat." [1]

The first of Oliver Wendell Holmes's novels, as we have seen, treated of the influence of extra natural pre-natal influence on the life of a human being, while the second was concerned with the actual controlling influence of various ancestors on one descendant—a more familiar problem in heredity ; in the last of the series, we have a work treating of the influence on the after life of a man of an antipathy arising from a severe shock suffered during early childhood.

Maurice Kirkwood, the hero of *A Mortal Anti-pathy*, was, as an infant, taken from his nurse's arms by a grown girl cousin so suddenly as to startle him into throwing himself from her arms over the parapet of the balcony on which they were. He was saved from death by falling into a rose-bush. The accident, however, so affected the

---

[1] *Merchant of Venice*, Act iv., sc. 1.

nerves of the child, that from that time he grew up with a "mortal antipathy" towards all womankind, and especially towards women at that time of life when they should naturally prove most attractive to the opposite sex. The antipathy is a purely physical one, for as he grows up to manhood, Maurice tries to reason himself out of it, but to no purpose. When he is by accident brought into the presence of a young woman, the result is invariably the same, a sudden faintness, which threatens to destroy his life. The consequence is that, with otherwise normally constituted social sympathies, he is yet compelled to lead an almost solitary life, merely on the borders of society. When the story commences—which is some time after the beginning of the book—he has taken up his residence near a small watering-place, Arrowhead Village, on the shore of a New England lake. He becomes, of course, an object of curiosity, and gives rise to much speculation among the Arrowhead inhabitants and visitors, more especially to some of the girl students at the Corinna Institute at the end of the lake. Two girls at the Institute more particularly interest themselves in the "Enigma." One of them, indeed, a very learned young lady known as "the Terror," from her way of carrying off all the prizes, so far interests herself as to determine to fathom the mystery surrounding the handsome young stranger.

The other of these two girls, "the Wonder," is so named on account of her great physical strength and athletic skill; from the first, the reader feels confident—such are the inexorable laws under which the novelist works—that Euthymia is not an Amazon in form and training to no purpose; and her strength is brought into play when Maurice Kirkwood is alone on a sick bed, helpless in a burning house; she fearlessly enters the building and carries him out, to life and safety—not alone from the fire, but also from his antipathy, for the severe shock and the method of his rescue serve to bring his organism back to a normal condition. The sequel is what might be expected.

The story is told with much amusing characterisation and much of the author's accustomed delightful gossip, but it is yet, as a whole, quite the least successful of Holmes's three novels. It is perhaps more "medicated" than either of its predecessors. It is more broken up with chapters and passages only partially pertinent to the story. The professional man is more than ever evident, philosophising over various matters more or less intimately connected with his art. The book is, however, charged with thought throughout, and is full of the amusing incidents and careful thought which go to the building up of each of our genial Autocrat's works.

A most amusing chapter describes a boat-race

between eight girls from the Institute and eight young students from the college at Arrowhead. Maurice Kirkwood in his canoe watches the race through field-glasses at a distance. The Terror is coxswain of her boat, with the Wonder as stroke. A stratagem on the part of the former, makes the girls victorious. When they are hard pressed by their opponents, Lurida throws a bunch of roses within reach of the coxswain of the boat ; he pauses momentarily to seize them.—

" The bow of the Algonquin passes the stern of the Atalanta !

" The bow of the Algonquin is on a level with the middle of the Atalanta !

" Three more lengths' rowing, and the college crew will pass the girls !

" ' Hurrah for the Quins ! ' The Algonquin ranges up alongside of the Atalanta !

" ' Through with her ! ' shouts the captain of the Algonquin.

" ' Now, girls ! ' shrieks the captain of the Atalanta.

" They near the line, every rower straining desperately, almost madly.

" Crack goes the oar of the Atalanta's captain, and up flash its splintered fragments, as the stem of her boat springs past the line, eighteen inches at least ahead of the Algonquin.

" ' Hooraw for the Lantas ! Hooraw for the

Girls ! Hooraw for the Institoot ! ' shout a hundred voices.

" ' Hurrah for woman's rights and female suffrage !' pipes the small voice of the Terror, and there is loud laughing and cheering all round.

" She had not studied her classical dictionary and her mythology for nothing. ' I have paid off one old score,' she said. ' Set down my damask roses against the golden apples of Hippomenes !'

" It was that one second lost in snatching up the bouquet which gave the race to the Atalantas." [1]

Of short, pertinent, and epigrammatic sayings and happy allusions, this one of the very latest of Holmes's works is as full as the earliest ones. One or two examples will suffice to indicate the quality of these sayings—" The rector maintained that physicians contracted a squint, which turns their eyes inwardly, while the muscles which roll their eyes upward become palsied. The doctor retorted that theological students developed a third eyelid—the *nictitating membrane*, which is so well known in birds, and which serves to shut out, not all light, but all the light they do not want."

" When gratitude is a bankrupt, love only can pay his debts."

" Wealth is a steep hill, which the father climbs

---

[1] *Mortal Antipathy*, p. 52.

slowly, and the son often tumbles down precipitately."

" I cannot help thinking that we carry our childhood's horizon with us all our days. . . . The ' clouds of glory ' which we trail with us in after life need not be traced to a pre-natal state."

In his reminiscent introduction to this story Holmes very happily describes N. P. Willis as " something between a remembrance of Count D'Orsay and an anticipation of Oscar Wilde."

These three novels, to sum up, are all more remarkable as character studies, and as the forcible literary expression of important and curious psychological and physiological problems than as dramatic creations. They are none of them, however, so exclusively this as to destroy our interest in the story, although it cannot be denied that that interest is lessened by the didactic object of the volumes—in other words, the moral has been pointed at the expense of art.

IV.

THE AUTOCRAT AND TEACHER.

THE AUTOCRAT.

(Read at the Holmes' Breakfast, Dec. 3, 1879.)

BY J. G. WHITTIER.

HIS laurels fresh from song and lay,
    Romance, art, science, rich in all,
And young of heart, how dare we say
    We keep his seventieth festival?

No sense is here of loss or lack;
    Before his sweetness and his light
The dial holds its shadow back,
    The charmèd hours delay their flight.

His still the keen analysis
    Of men and moods, electric wit,
Free play of mirth, and tenderness
    To heal the slightest wound from it.

And his the pathos touching all
    Life's sins and sorrows and regrets,
Its hopes and fears, its final call
    And rest beneath the violets.

His sparkling surface scarce betrays
    The thoughtful tide beneath it rolled —
The wisdom of the latter days,
    And tender memories of the old.

What shapes and fancies, grave or gay,
　　Before us at his bidding come !
The treadmill tramp, the One-Horse Shay,
　　The dumb despair of Elsie's doom !

The tale of Avis and the Maid,
　　The plea for lips that cannot speak,
The holy kiss that Iris laid
　　On Little Boston's pallid cheek !

Long may he live to sing for us
　　His sweetest songs at evening time,
And like his Chambered Nautilus,
　　To holier heights of beauty climb !

Though now unnumbered guests surround
　　The table that he rules at will,
Its Autocrat, however crowned,
　　Is but our friend and comrade still.

The world may keep his honoured name,
　　The wealth of all his varied powers;
A stronger claim has love than fame,
　　And he himself is only ours !

THE first four volumes of Holmes's collected writings belong to that side of his work for which he is at present, and will probably remain, most noted. As a poet, he may meet with the fate of those who treat chiefly of but occasional or humorous subjects; as a novelist, he may but have the temporary fame of one who writes with the object of pointing a present-day lesson ; as doctor and college professor, his work is of necessity of local interest though of long lasting import. None of these drawbacks attach to the four volumes of indescribable gossip which I have grouped together, in the title of this section, as the Autocrat. These are the books in which, over the breakfast-table and over the teacups, the Autocrat under his various aliases discourses on every subject that comes uppermost in conversation, or which he, as conversational leader, can initiate. The volumes are certainly most representative of all that is greatest and most original in the writings of Oliver Wendell Holmes—indeed, in the first three of them, the *Breakfast-Table Series*, we undoubtedly have him at his best. We have his rich witty style, his deep thought, his genial satire, his far-reaching discursiveness ranging over all subjects, his happy and entertaining wealth of illustration, along with his occasional gems of humour, pathos and poetry. It is all these combined qualities which go to make these volumes members of that small collection of best-loved books which most book-lovers have a tendency to form. Many of the qualities which make for the success of Doctor Holmes as Autocrat—I use this title, as I have hinted, for convenience, as inclusive of the others—are just those which militate, as we have seen, against the success of such single sustained effort as is required in a long story.

From its abrupt commencement, in 1857, in the

7

pages of the *Atlantic Monthly's* initial number, the *Autocrat of the Breakfast-Table* was hailed with delight; it has since become, with its later companion volumes, a recognised classic in the world of *belles-lettres*.

It was an audacious, though, as it proved, happy, idea of the author to thinly disguise himself and then dogmatise on all matters through a series of volumes; for the boarders around the table are scarcely ever allowed a word, and if they are it is only, as in the Platonic dialogues, as a leading up to some utterance of the principal speaker. Our knowledge of the Autocrat's satellites is gathered less from what they say than from what he says of them in his numerous asides to the reader. It was because it so very admirably suited the style of his genius that it was a happy audacity of Doctor Holmes, who, unequalled literary Autolycus, here provides us with philosophy and literature, æsthetics and humour, moral maxims and general criticism, with as ready a lavishness as ever the famous pedlar offered his miscellaneous wares. It has been objected against the Autocrat that he is too didactic, too prone to sermonise; but the occasional tendency towards this is far outweighed by the satire, wit and wisdom which play over the pages on all subjects, from that of the Universe to Lord Timothy Dexter. Among those few discursive books which charm us on account of their "style," their egotism, their very discursiveness—on the same shelf, that is, with Montaigne, Bacon, Walton, Fuller, Sir Thomas Browne and Elia—we may find fitting companionship for the breakfast-table trinity of Autocrat-Professor-Poet, " three starveling volumes bound in one."

The commencement of the second section of the *Autocrat* is delightful in pointing, with a very happy illustration, precisely what it is that the author does in his thoughtful, witty talks in type, as these papers may be termed.—" I really believe some people save their bright thoughts as being too precious for conversation. What do you think an admiring friend said the other day to one that was talking good things,—good enough to print ? ' Why,' said he, ' you are wasting mer-chantable literature, a cash article, at the rate, as nearly as I can tell, of fifty dollars an hour.' The talker took him to the window and asked him to look out and tell what he saw.

" ' Nothing but a very dusty street,' he said, ' and a man driving a sprinkling-machine through it.' ·

" ' Why don't you tell the man he is wasting that water ? What would be the state of the highways of life, if we did not drive our *thought-sprinklers* through them with the valves open, sometimes ?

" ' Besides, there is another thing about this

talking, which you forget. It shapes our thoughts for us;—the waves of conversation roll them as the surf rolls the pebbles on the shore. Let me modify the image a little. I rough out my thoughts in talk as an artist models in clay. Spoken language is so plastic,—you can pat and coax, and spread and shave, and rub out, and fill up, and stick on so easily, when you work that soft material, that there is nothing like it for modelling. Out of it come the shapes which you turn into marble or bronze in your immortal books, if you happen to write such. Or, to use another illustration, writing or printing is like shooting with a rifle; you may hit your reader's mind, or miss it;—but talking is like playing at a mark with the pipe of an engine; if it is within reach, and you have time enough, you can't help hitting it.' " [1] The Autocrat's "thought-sprinkler" is incessantly at work; while it is, undoubtedly, his use in writing of the full play of conversational freedom which makes him so often hit the mark at which he aims.

" It is very difficult," said an early reviewer of the *Autocrat*, and every critic must " echo the conceit," " to describe that which defies description." It is. And now, with the critic's accustomed confidence having pronounced a thing impossible,

---

[1] *The Autocrat*, pp. 27-8.

let me attempt its performance. It is, perhaps, easier to indicate what these books are by quotation from them than to describe them in a definition. In all four volumes we have Holmes, disguised as we have seen, talking in type with severe yet kindly satire, with wit " as polished and supple as a Damascus blade." Month after month for four different years, the last separated by nearly thirty years from the first, did he keep up the flow of his delightful talks. To turn, again, to his pages for an illustration—" The whole force of conversation depends on how much you can take for granted. Vulgar chess-players have to play their game out; nothing short of the brutality of an actual checkmate satisfies their dull apprehensions. But look at two masters of that noble game ! White stands well enough, so far as you can see ; but Red says, Mate in six moves ;—White looks,—nods ;—the game is over. Just so in talking with first-rate men ; especially when they are good-natured and expansive, as they are apt to be at table. That blessed clairvoyance which sees into things without opening them,—that glorious licence, which, having shut the door and driven the reporter from its keyhole, calls upon Truth, majestic virgin ! to get down from her pedestal and drop her academic poses, and take a festive garland and the vacant place on the *medius lectus*, —that carnival-shower of questions and replies and

comments, large axioms bowled over the mahogany
like bomb-shells from professional mortars, and
explosive wit dropping its trains of many-coloured
fire, and the mischief-making rain of *bon-bons*
pelting everybody that shows himself,—the picture
of a truly intellectual banquet is one which the
old Divinities might well have attempted to
reproduce in one of their——

"'Oh, oh, oh !' cried the young fellow whom they
call John,—'that is from one of your lectures !'

"'I know it, I replied,—I concede it, I confess
it, proclaim it.

"'The trail of the serpent is over them all !'

"All lecturers, all professors, all schoolmasters,
have ruts and grooves in their minds into which
their conversation is perpetually sliding."[1]

"Questions and replies and comments, large
axioms bowled over the mahogany"; the sentence
might stand as a motto to the four volumes; the
whole passage applies admirably to the conversation
of the Autocrat in all of his Protean performances
in these gossip-volumes. We have questions, replies and comments on all kinds of subjects in all
manner of styles—treating now of the fascinating
mysteries of life and death in the strain of a poet,
and again of hats in the manner of a humorist.
—"When we think of the familiar confidences of

---

[1] *The Autocrat*, pp. 64-5.

the Autocrat," says a critic, "we might liken him to Montaigne. But when the parallel is being considered we come upon passages so full of tingling hits or rollicking fun that we are sure we are mistaken, and that he resembles no one so much as Sydney Smith." Let us contrast, for example, the widely differing styles of the following passages culled almost at random. First we have a poetic-reminiscent passage, suggestive of no other writer so much as of Charles Lamb,—"Ah me! what strains and strophes of unwritten verse pulsate through my soul when I open a certain closet in the ancient house where I was born! On its shelves used to lie bundles of sweet-marjoram and pennyroyal and lavender and mint and catnip; there apples were stored until their seeds should grow black, which happy period there were sharp little milk-teeth always ready to anticipate; there peaches lay in the dark, thinking of the sunshine they had lost, until, like the hearts of saints who dream of heaven in their sorrow, they grew fragrant as the breath of angels. The odorous echo of a score of dead summers lingers yet in those dim recesses."[1] Let us then refer to the *Poet*, and read such a clinching statement as this :—" These people have always been shy of the astronomers,—they were shy, you know, of the

[1] *The Autocrat*, p. 78.

Copernican system, for a long while; well they might be with an *oubliette* waiting for them if they ventured to think that the earth moved round the sun. Science settled that point finally for them, at length, and then it was all right, —when there was no use in disputing the fact any longer. By-and-by geology began turning up fossils that told extraordinary stories about the duration of life upon our planet. What subterfuges were not used to get rid of their evidence! Think of a man seeing the fossilised skeleton of an animal split out of a quarry, his teeth worn down by mastication, and the remains of food still visible in his interior, and, in order to get rid of a piece of evidence contrary to the traditions he holds to, seriously maintaining that this skeleton never belonged to a living creature, but was created with just those appearances; a make-believe, a sham, a Barnum's-mermaid contrivance to amuse its Creator and impose upon His intelligent children! And now people talk about geological epochs and hundreds of millions of years in the planet's history as calmly as if they were discussing the age of their deceased great-grandmothers. Ten or a dozen years ago,[1] people said Sh! Sh! if you ventured to meddle with any question supposed to involve a doubt of the generally ac-

---

[1] This was written, it must be borne in mind, in 1872.

cepted Hebrew traditions. To-day such questions are recognised as perfectly fair subjects for general conversation ; not in the basement story, perhaps, or among the rank and file of the curbstone congregations, but among intelligent and educated persons. You may preach about them in your pulpit, you may lecture about them, you may talk about them with the first sensible-looking person you happen to meet, you may write magazine articles about them, and the editor need not expect to receive remonstrance from angry subscribers and withdrawals of subscriptions, as he would have been sure to not a great many years ago. Why, you may go to a tea-party where the clergyman's wife shows her best cap and his daughters display their shining ringlets, and you will hear the company discussing the Darwinian theory of the origin of the human race as if it were as harmless a question as that of the lineage of a spinster's lapdog. You may see a fine lady who is as particular in her genuflections as any Buddhist or Mahometan saint in his manifestations of reverence, who will talk over the anthropoid ape, the supposed founder of the family to which we belong, and even go back with you to the acephalous mollusk, first cousin to the clams and mussels, whose rudimental spine was the hinted prophecy of humanity ; all this time never dreaming, apparently, that what she takes for a matter of curious speculation involves the whole future of human progress and destiny." [1]

Or, taking up *The Professor*, we find a passage in which observation, thought, humour and sly sarcastic reproof are delightfully blent :—" I find that there is a very prevalent opinion among the dwellers on the shores of Sir Isaac Newton's Ocean of Truth, that *salt fish*, which have been taken from it a good while ago, split open, cured and dried, are the only proper and allowable food for reasonable people. I maintain, on the other hand, that there are a number of live fish still swimming in it, and that every one of us has a right to see if he cannot catch some of them. Sometimes I please myself with the idea that I have landed an actual living fish, small, perhaps, but with rosy gills and silvery scales. Then I find the consumers of nothing but the salted and dried article insist that it is poisonous, simply because it is alive, and cry out to people not to touch it. I have not found, however, that people mind them much." [2]

It is true, we may recognise a similarity between Holmes and Sydney Smith ; not alone on account of the "tingling hits," but also on account of the wonderful blending of the truest wisdom with the brightest wit. The Autocrat has himself recognised

---

[1] *The Poet*, pp. 180-2.   [2] *The Professor*, pp. 92-3.

what a dangerous thing it is for a literary man to indulge in a love of the ridiculous, which he may possess. " People laugh *with* him just so long as he amuses them ; but if he attempts to be serious, they must still have their laugh, and so they laugh *at* him." Once a funny man, always a funny man. Sydney Smith himself is a leading example ; the man who could write as he *did* write in the *Edinburgh Review* and in *Peter Plymley's Letters*, the Churchman, who was yet one of the staunchest supporters of an enlightened religious freedom, a Catholic emancipator, when such were all too few —this man is known to his contemporaries' grandchildren, almost exclusively as " a diner-out," " a joker of jokes," " a wit of the first water." He was all these, but he was, also, very much more. Smith is far from being a solitary example of this treatment of a great writer by posterity. To give a man the name of wit, as a wit himself has said, is as fatal as to give a dog a bad name. It would be a great loss to serious, thoughtful, literature, if Doctor Holmes's humour were allowed to eclipse his really greater work. He is undoubtedly a philosopher, and it would indeed be regretable that we should ignore his philosophy, while we applauded his fun.[1] These volumes are

---

[1] I have recently heard one critic put this case very strongly : he stated that, had the *Breakfast-Table Series* been minus eighty per cent. of its humour, it would have

full of true gems of thought on all questions concerned with the conduct of life. Doctor Holmes's religion, we have seen, is, so far as it is listable at all, a kind of broad Unitarianism; his philosophy is thoroughly optimistic; he does not, it is true, say that all is for the best in this best of all possible worlds, but he does point out that there is always a best which we may make our own. The wisdom of these volumes is really startling both in its wealth in point of quantity, and in its fulness of meaning in point of quality. Profound or suggestive utterances on all subjects are found scattered throughout. Often, however,—and it is to this that some readers object,—this thoughtful writing is "sandwiched in" between passages either of wild humour or impertinent interruption on the part of "the young man called John" or another of the boarders.

These books are admirably fitted, on account of the broad humanitarianism of the Autocrat, to be companion volumes to men and women of most diverse tastes and opinions, from those who read merely for amusement,—probably a vast majority, —to those who seek chiefly for stimulating thoughts. It is the great catholicity of the author's knowledge and interests, that doubtless gained for the work

at once been widely recognised as containing that great amount of wisdom now, to many readers, eclipsed by "fun" throughout.

such instant and such wide acceptance. With a university training, he studied first for the law, and afterwards for medicine; he practised as a physician, and as scientific professor; he had travelled—while, as a ground for the various knowledge thus attained by a penetrating, inquisitive mind in all these conditions, he had been born into and brought up in a minister's family. The result of this study of life from so many points of view, on a mind naturally quick and imaginative, is that which we now recognise as characteristic of Oliver Wendell Holmes as writer.

It has become too much the fashion, nowadays, so soon as a man makes any considerable stir in the world—be the sphere in which he makes it what it may, that of poet or preacher, dramatist or novelist—to refer to his "teaching," his "message," as a something definite and concrete. It has become, perhaps, something more than a fashion, it has become a habit of mind, so that when we are about to consider a man and his work we naturally find ourselves asking—What is his message? Has he a message differing from those of writers and workers who have preceded him? If not, to what already established class of teachers does he belong, or what common message does he mainly insist upon? This has been for some time our position when considering poets and their works—now we are getting messages concocted from our novelists

and dramatists. The "messages" of Browning
and Tennyson are giving way to those of Meredith
and Ibsen. Art for art's sake meets with but scant
courtesy at the hands of the many. Any such
teaching as Doctor Holmes may have to convey to
his generation—and his position as teacher is surely
no secondary one—is spread over his writing in all
its branches, his poems, his novels, his medical
essays and—far from in the smallest degree—over
the Breakfast-Table series.

It is, perhaps, no particularly new message which
he has to impart, but yet, like his own "female
Katydid,"

> " He says an undisputed thing
> In such a solemn way,"

that he often succeeds in impressing a truth upon
his readers which has been placed before them
often enough before but in such a manner that it
has been easiest to ignore it. On questions con-
cerning religion, for example, the truth which he
points may have been insisted upon before, but he
succeeds in making the question clear by the point
of view from which he looks at it. There is a story
told of Sydney Smith to the effect that he once
proposed that Government should pay the Irish
Catholic priests.

"They would not take it," said Doctor Doyle.

"Do you mean to say that if every priest in
Ireland received to-morrow morning a Government

letter with a hundred pounds, first quarter of their year's income, that they would refuse it ? "

"Ah, Mr. Smith," said Doctor Doyle, "you've such a way of putting things."

It is the same with Doctor Holmes : he has "such a way of putting things."

The chief line of his teaching, so far as religion is concerned, might well be indicated by two stanzas of Whittier's—

> " I have no answer for myself or thee,
>   Save that I learned beside my mother's knee ;
>   ' All is of God that is, and is to be ;
>   And God is good.'"[1]

> " I pray the prayer of Plato old :
>   God make thee beautiful within,
>   And let thine eyes the good behold
>   In everything save sin !"[2]

Doctor Holmes long attended King's Chapel, Boston, and is considered one of the most liberal-minded of Unitarians.   As it is shown to us in his writings, his theology might certainly be summed up in those two lines of the Quaker poet's just quoted—

> " All is of God that is, or is to be,
>   And God is good."

When, in the year 1877, Dr. Holmes was acting as President of the Boston Unitarian Festival he repeated a list of theological beliefs which he felt

---

[1] *Trust.*   [2] *My Namesake.*

called upon to combat. This list may best be given here in his own words as illustrating his position in this regard.

"May I," he began, "without committing any one but myself, enumerate a few of the stumbling-blocks which still stand in the way of some who have many sympathies with what is called the liberal school of thinkers?

" The notion of sin as a transferable object. As philanthropy has ridded us of chattel slavery, so philosophy must rid us of chattel sin and all its logical consequences.

" The notion that what we call sin is anything else than inevitable, unless the Deity had seen fit to give every human being a perfect nature, and develop it by a perfect education.

" The oversight of the fact that all moral relations between man and his Maker are reciprocal, and must meet the approval of man's enlightened conscience before he can render true and heartfelt homage to the power that called him into being. And is not the greatest obligation to all eternity on the side of the greatest wisdom and the greatest power?

" The notion that the Father of mankind is subject to the absolute control of a certain malignant entity known under the false name of justice, or subject to any law such as would have made the father of the prodigal son meet him with an account-book and pack him off to jail, instead of welcoming him back and treating him to the fatted calf.

"The notion that useless suffering is in any sense a satisfaction for sin, and not simply an evil added to a previous one." [1]

As a supplement to these beliefs which Doctor Holmes strongly protested against, we may refer to a page of the *Professor*, where we are given a number of axiomatic sentences on matters connected with the subject here treated. They were written, according to the author, after seeing something of a great many kinds of folks.

— "Of a hundred people of each of the different leading religious sects, about the same proportion will be safe and pleasant persons to deal and to live with.

— "There are, at least, three real saints among the women to one among the men, in every denomination.

— "The spiritual standard of different classes I would reckon thus :—

1. The comfortably rich.
2. The decently comfortable.
3. The very rich, who are apt to be irreligious.
4. The very poor, who are apt to be immoral.

— "The cut nails of machine-divinity may be driven in, but they won't clinch.

— "The arguments which the greatest of our

[1] W. S. Kennedy, *Oliver Wendell Holmes*, pp. 262-3.

schoolmen could not refute were two : the blood in
men's veins, and the milk in women's breasts.

— " Humility is the first of the virtues—for other
people.

— " Faith always implies the disbelief of a lesser
fact in favour of a greater. A little mind often
sees the unbelief, without seeing the belief of a
large one. . . .

" Which seems to you nearest heaven, Socrates
drinking his hemlock, Regulus going back to the
enemy's camp, or that old New England divine
sitting comfortably in his study and chuckling
over his conceit of certain poor women, who had
been burned to death in his own town, going
' roaring out of one fire into another ' ? " [1]

The theological aspect of the works of a non-
theological writer is one on which nowadays
somewhat too much stress is often laid owing
largely, perhaps, to the growth of the "theological
problem" novel. At times, it is true, lay writers
thrust their theology or no theology at us through
their novels with a purpose ; but after all the
beliefs or no beliefs of a writer, except in so far as
they are really insisted upon in the writings,
should not concern his readers. What does it
matter to us that Montaigne was a Romanist, and
Fuller a Church of England divine, or what Charles

---

[1] *Professor*, pp. 121-2.

Lamb was, when we are reading their entertaining literary bequests? We are perhaps more justified in searching the works of a didactic writer like Holmes to acquaint ourselves with what may be his hopes and beliefs, his aspirations and religion. Throughout his writings we are conscious of a spirit of true reverence, though he speaks with scathing scorn, again and again, of any narrowing sects and creeds. Be religious, by all means, but be not blindly religious,—

" Be not like dumb driven cattle." [1]

Think and believe for yourself—let not others do the thinking and believing for you. As he pertinently expresses it, in the early pages of the *Professor*, " If a human soul is necessarily to be trained up in the faith of those from whom it inherits its body, why, there is the end of all reason. If, sooner or later, every soul is to look for truth with its own eyes, the first thing is to recognise that no presumption in favour of any particular belief arises from the fact of our inheriting it. Otherwise you would not give the Mahometan a fair chance to become a convert to a better religion." [2] The same idea has, of course, been stated before, notably, in the well-known lines—

---

[1] Longfellow, *Psalm of Life*. [2] *Professor*, p. 6.

> "Many a man
> Owes to his country his religion;
> And in another would as strongly grow,
> Had but his nurse and mother taught him so."

On the same page with the passage I have just
quoted, Doctor Holmes well says, in a sentence
fraught with deep meaning, " the religious cur-
rency of mankind, in thought, in speech, and in
print, consists entirely of polarised words."[1] That
is to say, words which have lain long in the mind
have undergone a change " like that which rest in
a certain position gives to iron "; they have become
magnetic in their relations and are traversed by
forces not belonging to them. This eminently
happy " way of putting things " is illustrated by
the use of the sacred word " O'm " from Hindoo
mythology, a word which it is a great sin to
pronounce. " What do you care for O'm? " the
Autocrat continues. " If you wanted to get the
Pundit to look at his religion fairly, you must first
depolarise this and all similar words for him.
The argument for and against new translations
of the Bible really turns on this. Scepticism is
afraid to trust its truths in depolarised words, and
so cries out against a new translation. I think,
myself, if every idea our Book contains could be
shelled out of its own symbol and put into a new,
clean, unmagnetic word, we should have some

---

[1] *Professor*, p. 6.

chance of reading it as philosophers, or wisdom-lovers, ought to read it,—which we do not and cannot now any more than a Hindoo can read the *Gayatri*, as a fair man and lover of truth should do. When society has once fairly dissolved the New Testament, which it never has done yet, it will perhaps crystallise it over again in new forms of language." [1]

This is but one of very many of the Autocrat's utterances on similar subjects—utterances which are extremely valuable on account of their great lucidity and suggestiveness. There is nothing narrowing and dogmatic in his teaching—" I have known and loved to talk with good people, all the way from Rome to Geneva in doctrine, as long as I can remember." [2] This passage shows the extreme tolerance of his view, which has been indicated earlier. Yet once again he says in the same volume, and in saying it, clinches for himself that sturdy independence of position which he looks upon as essential for all—" We are false to our new conditions of life, if we do not resolutely maintain our religious as well as our political freedom, in the face of any and all supposed monopolies. Certain men will, of course, say two things, if we do not take their views : first, that we don't know anything about these matters : and, secondly, that we

---

[1] *Professor*, p. 7.   [2] *Ibid.*, p. 124.

are not so good as they are. They have a polarised
phraseology for saying these things, but it comes
to precisely that. To which it may be answered,
in the first place, that we have good authority for
saying that even babes and sucklings know *something* ; and, in the second, that, if there is a mote
or so to be removed from our premises, the courts
and councils of the last few years have found
beams enough in some other quarters to build
a church that would hold all the good people in
Boston, and have sticks enough left to make a
bonfire for all the heretics." [1]

On other great questions we find the same clear
independent statement, and in his latest as in his
earlier works. In *Over the Teacups*, Doctor Holmes
gives an amusing abridged history of two worlds,
this and the next, thus,—

!

———

?

His interpretation of this hieroglyphic is as
follows :—

" Two worlds, the higher and the lower, separated
by the thinnest of partitions. The lower world is
that of questions; the upper world is that of
answers. Endless doubt and unrest here below ;

———

[1] *Professor*, pp. 125-6

wondering, admiring, adoring certainty above." [1]
This is amusing, but very far from conclusive.
Suppose we reverse the positions of the signs, we
should have—the lower world, an exclamation ;
—as Lord Byron says, " all present life is but an
interjection " [2]—and the higher world, what ? One
of his finest utterances on this question is to be
found in the concluding stanzas of *The Chambered
Nautilus,*—

"Thanks for the heavenly message brought by thee,
  　　Child of the wandering sea,
  　　Cast from her lap, forlorn!
From thy dead lips a clearer note is born
Than ever Triton blew from wreathéd horn! [3]
  　　While on mine ear it rings,
Through the deep caves of thought I hear a voice that
  　sings :—
Build thee more stately mansions, O my soul,
  　　As the swift seasons roll !
  　　Leave thy low-vaulted past !
Let each new temple, nobler than the last,
Shut thee from heaven with a dome more vast,
  　　Till thou at length art free,
Leaving thine outgrown shell by life's unresting sea!" [4]

The kindly treatment by the author of the poor,
hesitating, doubting Reverend Mr. Chauncey Fair-

---

[1] *Teacups*, p. 117.　　　　[2] *Don Juan*, Canto XV.
[3] This is, obviously, an echo of the concluding line of
Wordsworth's famous sonnet,—
  　　" The world is too much with us."
[4] *Poems*, ii., p. 108.

weather is but another aspect of that toleration towards all shades of belief which Doctor Holmes himself exercises. Indeed, in the scene in which Mr. Fairweather goes to Doctor Kittredge for advice, we feel that we have the writer himself—"a sermon by a lay-preacher may be worth listening to "[1]—addressing all who are hesitating, not so much between two opinions, as on the point of taking a step which they wish to take, but about which they fear to be severely criticised.[2] He says to them, even though you have gone so far with me, if you see cause to change your views do so. He feels for, and sympathises with, the convert from one belief to another—too often impudently dubbed pervert by those whom he leaves.

> " Deal meekly, gently, with the hopes that guide
> The lowliest brother straying from thy side:
> If right, they bid thee tremble for thine own;
> If wrong, the verdict is for God alone!"[3]

In the scene to which I have referred, between the minister drifting Rome-wards, and the dear, humane and sensible old medico, Doctor Holmes, with his usual clear way of seeing and saying things, points out how it is that men who see *into* others are apt to be contemptuous, while men who see *through* them find something behind each human

---

[1] *Professor*, p. 7.   [2] *Elsie Venner*, chap. 27.
[3] *Poems*, i., p. 119.

soul which it is not for them to sit in judgment upon nor to sneer at as out of the order of things.

The modern spirit in which Doctor Holmes treats of nineteenth-century scientific research and its resultant teaching was shown in the section devoted to his work as novelist. On one subject, which is a manifestation of the modern spirit brought to bear upon the conditions of human life, Doctor Holmes is curiously in harmony with two men who differ as widely from each other in manner as they both do from him. These men are Walt Whitman and Henrik Ibsen. In addressing a working men's club at Drontheim in 1885 the Norwegian dramatist said: "The revolution in the social condition, now preparing in Europe, is chiefly concerned with the future of the workers and the women. In this I place all my hopes and expectations; for this I will work with all my life and with all my strength."[1] While Whitman has numerous passages, such as this from the *Song of Myself,*—

" I am the poet of the woman the same as the man,
   And I say it is as great to be a woman as to be a man,
   And I say there is nothing greater than the mother of
      men." [2]

Doctor Holmes has frequent passages the idea

[1] *The Pillars of Society*, etc., edited by Havelock Ellis, p. xii.
[2] *Leaves of Grass : Song of Myself*, 21.

in which may claim kinship with that in the
utterances of Ibsen and Whitman.

> " Would that the heart of woman warmed our creeds !
> Not from the sad-eyed hermit's lonely cell,
> Not from the conclave where the holy men
> Glare on each other, as with angry eyes
> They battle for God's glory and their own,
> Till, sick of wordy strife, a show of hands
> Fixes the faith of ages yet unborn,—
> Ah, not from these the listening soul can hear
> The Father's voice that speaks itself divine !
> Love must be still our Master; till we learn
> What he can teach us of a woman's heart,
> We know not his whose love embraces all." [1]

And yet again he says, " I have been ready to
believe that we have even now a new revelation,
and the name of its Messiah is WOMAN !" [2] This
passage, written over thirty years ago, might be
called almost prophetic. For along with the oft-
times raucous cry of " woman's rights " has un-
questionably come a tendency more fittingly to
acknowledge woman's true sphere in civilised
society.

Throughout his writings Holmes is inculcating
the same lessons of self-reliant optimism—"we
carry happiness into our condition, but must not
expect to find it there." " To thine own self be
true," he says again and again; in other words, " If
you would be happy in Berkshire, you must carry

---

[1] *Poems*, ii., p. 195.   [2] *Professor*, p. 125.

mountains in your brain; and if you would enjoy
Nahant, you must have an ocean in your soul.
Nature plays at dominos with you; you must
match her piece, or she will never give it up to
you."[1] What an excellent way of putting what
has been said often enough, and never better,
perhaps, than in that epigram, " The eye sees
that which it brings with it the power of seeing."
What wholesome advice, too, is contained in the
whole of *A Rhymed Lesson*! How well pointed are
these lines addressed to " *Poor Richard's* fellow-
citizens " !—

> " Yet in opinions look not always back,—
>   Your wake is nothing, mind the coming track;
>   Leave what you've done for what you have to do;
>   Don't be ' consistent,' but be simply true.
>   Don't catch the fidgets; you have found your place
>   Just in the focus of a nervous race,
>   Fretful to change and rabid to discuss,
>   Full of excitements, always in a fuss.
>   Run, if you like, but try to keep your breath;
>   Work like a man, but don't be worked to death;
>   And with new notions,—let me change the rule,—
>   Don't strike the iron till it's slightly cool."[2]

" It isn't what a man thinks or says, but when
and where and to whom he thinks and says it."
I have heard it objected to Doctor Holmes that
he is guilty of saying what he thinks *not* at the
right moment, that, in fact, his didactic writing

[1] *Autocrat*, p. 265.   [2] *Poems*, i., pp. 121-2.

is out of place in humorous papers such as the
Breakfast-Table Series.   I must confess that when
I heard this I felt that the criticism of another
friend (referred to earlier, see p. 107) was justified,
that the volumes would be better—or more
properly—appreciated if they were minus a goodly
percentage of the humorous writing.   The lighter
style may, on the whole, predominate, but I should
imagine that the author set out not to write
humour, but to express his thoughts amid a
humorous setting, the better to get them read,
in the same manner as he set out in each of his
novels to discuss a definite psychological or
pathological problem.   In the former case the
teaching was probably much less definite even in
the mind of the author than in the latter.   Of
his listeners he says on one occasion, "I know
well enough that there are some of you who had
a great deal rather see me stand on my head
than use it for any purpose of thought. . . . Well,
I can't be savage with you for wanting to laugh,
and I like to make you laugh well enough, when I
can.   But then observe this : if the sense of the
ridiculous is one side of an impressible nature,
it is very well; but if that is all there is in a man,
he had better have been an ape at once, and so
have stood at the head of his profession."[1]   In

---

[1] *Autocrat,* p. 90.

defending his changeableness from serious thought
to entertaining humour, Holmes says, and gives
the quotation all the importance which capital
letters can impart, and at the same time gives us
a summing-up in brief of what his own teaching
may be said to represent,—" I know nothing in
English or any other literature more admirable
than that sentiment of Sir Thomas Browne,
' EVERY MAN TRULY LIVES, SO LONG AS HE ACTS HIS
NATURE, OR SOME WAY MAKES GOOD THE FACULTIES
OF HIMSELF.' "

A few words may here be devoted to the volume
of essays entitled *Pages from an Old Volume of
Life*, a volume which includes the very striking
address—*The Inevitable Trial*—to which I have
referred earlier, and also the beautiful quadruple
essay entitled *The Seasons*. In an all-too-short
chapter of reminiscence called *Cinders from the
Ashes*, Doctor Holmes tells of his early schooling
and of his early schoolfellows—some of whom had
since become famous, and describes how at the end
of August 1867, he made a sentimental journey to
old haunts at Andover. " The ghost of a boy was
at my side as I wandered among the places he
knew so well. I went to the front of the house.
There was the great rock showing its broad back
in the front yard. *I used to crack nuts on that*,
whispered the small ghost. I looked in at the
upper window in the farther part of the house. *I*

looked out of that on four long changing seasons,
said the ghost. . . . And here is the back road
that will lead me round by the old Academy
building. Could I believe my senses when I found
that it was turned into a gymnasium, and heard
the low thunder of ninepin-balls, and the crash of
tumbling pins from those precincts? The little
ghost said, *Never! It cannot be.* But it was.
' Have they a billiard-room in the upper story?' I
asked myself. Do the theological professors take
a hand at all-fours or poker on week-days, now and
then, and read the secular column of the *Boston
Recorder* on Sundays? I was demoralised for the
moment, it is plain; but now that I have recovered
from the shock, I must say that the fact mentioned
seems to show a great advance in common sense
from the notions prevailing in my time." [1]

Thus round all the old spots teeming with associa-
tions goes the man accompanied by the ghost of his
boyhood until it is time to return, when——"' Two
tickets to Boston,' I said to the man at the station.

" But the little ghost whispered, *When you leave
this place you leave me behind you.*

"' *One* ticket to Boston, if you please. Good-bye,
little ghost.'

" I believe the boy-shadow still lingers around
the well-remembered scenes I traversed on that

---

[1] *Pages from an Old Volume of Life,* pp. 254–5.

day, and that, whenever I revisit them, I shall
find him again as my companion."[1]

The whole of this volume of *Pages* is made up of
eminently instructive, thoughtful, and at the same
time entertaining matter, varied it is true as
may be seen from a glance at the contents from
papers such as that from which I have just quoted
to such subjects as *Crime and Automatism* and
Mechanism in Thought and Morals. This last-
mentioned essay was delivered as an address before
the Phi Beta Kappa Society in 1870.[2] Its line of
thought may be guessed at once from that of the
novels which we have already considered. It is,
in a measure, a re-stating of the same problems
which had fascinated the author earlier, and
should be read by all who take an interest in
questions of morals and individual responsibility.
Doctor Holmes claims that a large part of our
mental as of our physical life is mechanical, that
is, independent of our volition, and goes on to say
that " our natural instincts and tastes have a basis
which can no more be reached by the will than
the sense of light and darkness or that of heat
and cold."[3] Later on in the essay the author
illustrates in a very happy manner the position

---

[1] *Pages from an Old Volume of Life*, pp. 258-9.
[2] This paper is published as a small volume, apart from
the *Works*, both in England and America.
[3] *Pages from an Old Volume of Life*, p. 261.

which he takes up. "The misfortune of perverse instincts, which adhere to us as congenital inheritances, should go to our side of the account, if the books of heaven are kept, as the great Church of Christendom maintains they are, by double entry. But the absurdity which has been held up to ridicule in the nursery has been enforced as the highest reason upon older children. Did our forefathers tolerate *Æsop* among them? 'I cannot trouble the water where you are,' says the lamb to the wolf: 'don't you see that I am farther down the stream?'—'But a year ago you called me ill-names.'—'Oh, sir! a year ago I was not born!'—'Sirrah,' replies the wolf, 'if it wasn't you it was your father, and that is all one,' and finishes with the usual practical application." [1]

---

[1] *Pages from an Old Volume of Life*, pp. 304-5.

V.

THE DOCTOR.

VERSES.

(Read at the Complimentary Dinner given to Dr. Holmes by the Medical Profession of New York on April 12, 1883.)

By Dr. A. H. Smith.

You've heard of the deacon's one-hoss shay
Which, finished in Boston the self-same day
That the city of Lisbon went to pot,
Did a century's service and then was not.
But the record's at fault which says that it bust
Into simply a heap of amorphous dust,
For after the wreck of that wonderful tub
Out of the ruins they saved a hub;
And the hub has since stood for Boston town,
Hub of the Universe, note that down.
But an orderly hub, as all will own,
Must have something central to turn upon,
And, rubber cushioned, and true and bright,
We have the axle here to-night.
Thrice welcome then to our festal board
The doctor-poet, so doubly stored
With science as well as with native wit,
Poeta nascitur, you know, *non fit*,
Skilled to dissect with knife or pen—
His subjects dead or living men;

With thought sublime on every page
To swell the veins with virtuous rage,
Or with a syringe to inject them
With sublimate, to disinfect them;
To show with demonstrator's art
The complex chambers of the heart;
Or armed with a diviner skill
To make it pulsate at his will;
With generous verse to celebrate
The loaves and fishes of some giver;
And then proceed to demonstrate
The lobes and fissures of the liver;
To soothe the pulses of the brain
With poetry's enchanting strain,
Or to describe to class uproarious
Pes hippocampi accessorious;
To nerve with fervour of appeal
The sluggish muscles into steel,
Or, pulling their attachments, show
Whence they arise and where they go;
To fire the eye by wit consummate,
Or draw the aqueous humour from it;
In times of peril give the tone
To public feeling, called backbone,
Or to discuss that question solemn,
The muscles of the spinal column.
And now I close my artless ditty
As per agreement with committee,
And making place for those more able
I leave the subject on the table.

IN this presentment of the life and work of Oliver
Wendell Holmes as a literary man it is not
necessary to treat at any length of his work as
a scientist—as student, physician and professor;

except in so far as that scientific work and knowledge have influenced or coloured the literary work, and this has already been done incidentally in the preceding pages.

On returning from his European studies, and taking his medical degree, as we saw earlier, young Doctor Holmes distinguished himself by carrying off three out of four medals offered for essays on certain medical subjects. These essays were published in 1838, but have not been included by the author in his collected writings, though he tells us in a " Second Preface " to the volume of *Medical Essays* that he felt tempted to include the Essay on *Intermittent Fever in New England*. The essays which he has included in this volume are named the list at the conclusion of this book. As Professor of Anatomy and Physiology, first at Dartmouth and then, for upwards of thirty years, at Harvard, Holmes's influence for good must have been incalculable. A man thoroughly versed in the branches of science which it was his province to teach, of keen insight into facts, both of character and of knowledge, gifted with a remarkable power of literary expression, with an epigrammatically clear and concise way of putting things, of wide culture, in keen sympathy with those whom he was teaching, and of strong personal charm, it is difficult to conceive of a man more fitted for the *rôle* of teacher.

Several of the essays in *Pages from an Old Volume of Life* are inspired by the author's professional studies; essays such as those on the *Physiology of Walking* and *of Versification.* We shall, however, best know the doctor-writer in the volume which he has named *Medical Essays.* The first paper in this book is on *Homœopathy and its Kindred Delusions,* and in it Doctor Holmes treats to " critical martyrdom " a craze which he says is not entitled, by anything it has done or said, to even so much notoriety as a public rebuke. This essay was delivered, in the form of two lectures, before the Boston Society for the Diffusion of General Knowledge. Needless to say that it was treated to many " counterblasts " from the voices and pens of the followers of Samuel Hahnemann. Doctor Holmes cited cases and references innumerable proving the delusion under which the supporters of Homœopathy were labouring. " Not one statement shall be made which cannot be supported by unimpeachable reference. . . . I have no quibbles to utter, and shall stoop to answer none ; but, with full faith in the sufficiency of a plain statement of facts and reasons, I submit the subject." [1] The following is an amusing example of the cases cited by the indignant attacker of Homœopathy. " A young woman affected with

---

[1] *Medical Essays,* p. 40.

jaundice is mentioned in the German *Annals of Clinical Homœopathy* as having been cured in twenty-nine days by pulsatilla and nux vomica. Rummel, a well-known writer of the same school, speaks of curing a case of jaundice in thirty-four days by Homœopathic doses of pulsatilla, aconite, and cinchona. I happened to have a case in my own household a few weeks since, which lasted about ten days, and this was longer than I have repeatedly seen it in hospital practice, so that it was nothing to boast of."[1] This case well points the one valuable thing which Doctor Holmes finds that Homœopathy has taught,—namely, the wonderful restorative and curative power of Nature herself, a power which, by the way, Hahnemann and his disciples explicitly deny. With regard to the survival of Homœopathy at all, Doctor Holmes says, leaving his readers to supply italics to the latter half of his sentence, "It takes time for truth to operate as well as Homœopathic globules."[2] Throughout a hundred pages the doctor adduces arguments, cases and reasons against this delusion, and treats it to the scorn and sarcasm of which he is no insignificant master. His opposition to Homœopathy is again shown in the latest of his volumes, *Our Hundred Days in Europe*. Indeed, he tells us that when at Stratford-on-Avon he had to change

---

[1] *Medical Essays*, pp. 76-7.   [2] *Ibid.*, p. 78.

his room at the hotel, because the window of the first one which was given to him looked straight across the street at a chemist's shop where was displayed a large cast of the head of the "old humbug" Hahnemann. The *Essay* first spoken of is thus summed up:—"Such is the pretended science of Homœopathy, to which you are asked to trust your lives and the lives of those dearest to you. A mingled mass of perverse ingenuity, of tinsel erudition, of imbecile credulity, and of artful misrepresentation, too often mingled in practice, if we may trust the authority of its founder, with heartless and shameless imposition. Because it is suffered so often to appeal unanswered to the public, because it has its journals, its patrons, its apostles, some are weak enough to suppose it can escape the inevitable doom of utter disgrace and oblivion. Not many years can pass away before the same curiosity excited by one of Perkins's Tractors will be awakened at the sight of one of the Infinitesimal Globules. If it should claim a longer existence, it can only be by falling into the hands of the sordid wretches who wring their bread from the cold grasp of disease and death in the hovels of ignorant poverty." [1]

The essay on *The Contagiousness of Puerperal Fever*, is probably the most valuable contribution

---

[1] *Medical Essays*, p. 101.

to medical literature which Doctor Holmes has made. It was no new theory which he pressed forward—now just half a century since [1]—but an eloquent insistence upon a fact which, while carelessly overlooked by the majority of practitioners, was even denied by one or two leading men in the profession. This paper, proving conclusively the contagiousness which had already been imagined, roused a wider attention to the facts of the case.

In *Currents and Counter Currents*, addressed (1860) to the members of the Massachusetts Medical Society, we have a plea, practically, for less medicine and more sanitation; a little more prevention, that attempted cure may be unnecessary —it is so much simpler to take the button from the child before he has swallowed it than after. The essay constitutes a claim for medicine, that it shall not necessarily follow the lines of Galen and Hippocrates, because at one time those lines were the best known; that the physician shall not recommend calomel, because, like the landlord when he recommends eggs and bacon, " it is handy." This essay contains, also, passages reminiscent of the two preceding ones, showing that the author still felt as strongly as ever on the subjects therein considered. One sly reference to Hahnemann is amusing :—" I confess that I should think my chance of recovery from illness less with Hippo-

---

[1] The paper was first printed in 1843.

crates for my physician and Mrs. Gamp for my
nurse, than if I were in the hands of Hahnemann
himself, with Florence Nightingale or good Rebecca
Taylor to care for me." [1]

The third essay in this volume is especially interesting to students of Holmes's works ; it is entitled
Border Lines in Medical Science, and was delivered
as the introductory lecture to the medical class of
Harvard in 1861. In it the author says that his
task is " only that of sending out a few pickets
under the starry flag of science to the edge of that
dark domain where the ensigns of the obstinate
rebel, Ignorance, are flying undisputed." [2] Much
of Doctor Holmes's writing may be said to take us
to the border line of science, not so much on the
side of ignorance, as on the side of the partially
known. We feel that, though treating of various
abstruse problems in his novels, for example, he is
yet of that minority which we have been recently
taught to believe " is always right." He is with
the very advanced guard of thinkers on the border
line, and the messages which he sends back to the
main column, although at first, perhaps, scouted
and disbelieved, are none the less true therefore.

In a valedictory address to a class of graduating
students—*The Young Practitioner*—Doctor Holmes
gives some excellent advice, pointed with all his
accustomed humour; again he insists upon a

---

[1] *Medical Essays,* p. 204.   [2] *Ibid.,* p. 212.

matter to which he refers several times elsewhere, the duty of a physician *not* to tell a patient the truth, the whole truth and nothing but the truth.

"Your patient has no more right to all the truth you know than he has to all the medicine in your saddlebags, if you carry that kind of cartridge-box for the ammunition that slays disease. He should get only just so much as is good for him. I have seen a physician examining a patient's chest stop all at once, as he brought out a particular sound with a tap on the collar-bone, in the attitude of a pointer who has just come on the scent or sight of a woodcock. You remember that Spartan boy, who, with unmoved countenance, hid the fox that was tearing his vitals beneath his mantle. What he could do in his own suffering you must learn to do for others on whose vital organs disease has fastened its devouring teeth. It is a terrible thing to take away hope, even earthly hope, from a fellow-creature. Be very careful what names you let fall before your patient. He knows what it means when you tell him he has tubercles or Bright's disease, and, if he hears the word carcinoma, he will certainly look it out in a medical dictionary, if he does not interpret its dread significance on the instant. Tell him he has asthmatic symptoms, or a tendency to the gouty diathesis, and he will at once think of all the asthmatic and gouty old patriarchs he has

ever heard of, and be comforted. You need not
be so cautious in speaking of the health of rich
and remote relatives, if he is in the line of
succession." [1]

The essay on *Medical Libraries* is valuable, not
alone to medical readers—indeed none of these
papers appeal purely to specialists—but to all as a
delightful gossip about books, with some excellent
remarks on the subject of indexing. Just as we
found the doctor colouring the work of the poet and
novelist, so we find the poet and novelist in their
turn contributing something to the medical papers
—which papers are hence very pleasant reading to
all. One of the students of Doctor Holmes's last
class at Harvard, in speaking of his influence as
lecturer, points very well the influence which, in
virtue of the same qualities, he exercises over his
readers. " We always " (wrote this student) " welcomed Professor Holmes with enthusiastic cheers
when he came into the class-room, and his lectures
were so brimful of anecdote that we sometimes
forgot it was a lesson in anatomy we had come to
learn. But the instruction—deep, sound, and
thorough—was there all the same, and we never
left the room without feeling what a fund of knowledge and what a clear insight upon difficult points
in medical science had been imparted to us through
the sparkling medium."

---

[1] *Medical Essays*, pp. 388-9.

THE IRON GATE.

By Oliver Wendell Holmes.

WHERE is this patriarch you are kindly greeting?
  Not unfamiliar to my ear his name,
Nor yet unknown to many a joyous meeting
  In days long vanished,—is he still the same,

Or changed by years, forgotten and forgetting,
  Dull-eared, dim-sighted, slow of speech and
    thought,
Still o'er the sad, degenerate present fretting,
  Where all goes wrong, and nothing as it ought?

Old age, the greybeard! Well, indeed, I know
    him,—
  Shrunk, tottering, bent, of aches and ills the prey;
In sermon, story, fable, picture, poem,
  Oft have I met him from my earliest day:

In my old Æsop, toiling with his bundle,—
  His load of sticks,—politely asking Death,
Who comes when called for,—would he lug or
    trundle
  His fagot for him?—he was scant of breath.

And sad "Ecclesiastes, or the Preacher,"—
  Has he not stamped the image on my soul,
In that last chapter, where the worn-out Teacher
  Sighs o'er the loosened cord, the broken bowl ?

Yes, long, indeed, I've known him at a distance,
  And now my lifted door-latch shows him here ;
I take his shrivelled hand without resistance,
  And find him smiling as his step draws near.

What though of gilded baubles he bereaves us,
  Dear to the heart of youth, to manhood's prime ;
Think of the calm he brings, the wealth he leaves
    us,
  The hoarded spoils, the legacies of time !

Altars once flaming, still with incense fragrant,
  Passions uneasy nurslings rocked asleep,
Hope's anchor faster, wild desire less vagrant,
  Life's flow less noisy, but the stream how deep !

Still as the silver cord gets worn and slender,
  Its lightened task-work tugs with lessening strain,
Hands get more helpful, voices, grown more tender,
  Soothe with their softened tones the slumberous
    brain.

Youth longs and manhood strives, but age remem-
    bers,
  Sits by the raked-up ashes of the past,
Spreads its thin hands above the whitening embers
  That warm its creeping life-blood till the last.

Dear to its heart is every loving token
  That comes unbidden ere its pulse grows cold,
Ere the last lingering ties of life are broken,
  Its labours ended and its story told.

Ah, while around us rosy youth rejoices,
  For us the sorrow-laden breezes sigh,
And through the chorus of its jocund voices
  Throbs the sharp note of misery's hopeless cry.

As on the gauzy wings of fancy flying
  From some far orb I track our watery sphere,
Home of the struggling, suffering, doubting, dying,
  The silvered globule seems a glistening tear.

But Nature lends her mirror of illusion
  To win from saddening scenes our age-dimmed
    eyes,
And misty day-dreams blend in sweet confusion
  The wintry landscape and the summer skies.

So when the iron portal shuts behind us,
  And life forgets us in its noise and whirl,
Visions that shunned the glaring noonday find us,
  And glimmering starlight shows the gates of
    pearl.

I come not here your morning hour to sadden,
  A limping pilgrim, leaning on his staff,—
I, who have never deemed it sin to gladden
  This vale of sorrow with a wholesome laugh.

If word of mine another's gloom has brightened,
  Through my dumb lips the heaven-sent message
    came ;
If hand of mine another's task has lightened,
  It felt the guidance that it dares not claim.

But, O my gentle sisters, O my brothers,
  These thick-sown snow-flakes hint of toil's
    releas‹
These feebler pulses bid me leave to others
  The tasks once welcome ; evening asks for peace.

Time claims his tribute ; silence now is golden ;
  Let me not vex the too-long-suffering lyre ;
Though to your love untiring still beholden,
  The curfew tells me—cover up the fire.

And now with grateful smile and accents cheerful,
  And warmer heart than look or word can tell,
In simplest phrase—these traitorous eyes are
    tearful—
  Thanks, Brothers, Sisters,—Children,—and fare-
    well !

www.ingramcontent.com/pod-product-compliance
Lightning Source LLC
Chambersburg PA
CBHW021137020726
47500CB00003B/1116